THE TAKING OF

EDEN

By
Robin Alexander

THE TAKING OF EDEN
© 2005 BY ROBIN ALEXANDER

ISBN: 978-1-933113-53-1

CREDITS

EXECUTIVE EDITOR: TARA YOUNG
COVER DESIGN BY SHERI (GRAPHICARTIST2020@HOTMAIL.COM)

Published by
Intaglio Publications
P O Box 357474
Gainesville, Florida 32635

Visit us on the web: www.intagliopub.com

Other Books by Robin Alexander

Gloria's Inn

Hayden Tate suddenly found herself in a world unlike any other, when she inherited half of an inn nestled away on Cat Island in the Bahamas. Expecting something like the resorts found in Nassau, Hayden was shocked and a little disappointed to find herself on a beautiful tropical island undiscovered by tourism. Hayden reluctantly begins to adapt to a simpler way of life found on the island, and her conversion is often comical.

Not only did Hayden's aunt leave her an inn, but the company of her former business partner, as well. Strange as she is beautiful, Adrienne turns Hayden's world upside down in many ways. Hayden quickly learns that being with Adrienne will always be an adventure.

The tranquility of the island is shattered with the disappearance of a mysterious guest. Hayden and Adrienne find themselves at the center of a murder investigation, fearing for their own safety and the lives of their guests. Eager to rid themselves and the island of a ruthless killer, Adrienne and Hayden decide to conduct their own investigation. The eclectic mixture of guests and staff make their efforts interesting and humorous.

Murky Waters

Claire Murray thought she was leaving her problems behind when she accepted a new position within Suarez Travel and relocated to Baton Rouge. Her excitement quickly diminishes when her mysterious stalker makes it known that there is no place Claire can hide. She is instantly attracted to the enigmatic Tristan Delacroix, who becomes more of a mystery to her every time they meet. Claire is thrust into a world of fear, confusion, and passion that will ultimately shake the foundations of all she once believed.

Dedication

A truly gifted and dedicated nurse has the ability to provide compassionate care for an individual and also focus on the medical need of his or her patient. Normally, being the first face a patient sees, they often bear the brunt of agitation brought on by pain, fear, and confusion experienced by the patient and the family in a situation that is foreign in their day-to-day lives. Underappreciated and overworked nurses face these issues daily, and with grace and dignity, they persevere.

The inspiration for the character Jamie came from a very real neuro ICU nurse—my beloved sister-in-law. Listening to her stories of patients and seeing firsthand the effect it has on her emotionally, I am always amazed that she has the ability to shut herself away from the pain and horror and return each day to do the job she loves.

A resident of New Orleans, she lost her home and job to Hurricane Katrina. The familiarity of her workplace and the comfort of her home were taken from her in an instant. And yet, she still faces each day of uncertainty with an attitude that I'm not sure I could manage under the circumstances.

Holly, you've become a very dear friend and someone I truly admire. You have my love, respect, and adoration always.
Robin

Acknowledgments

I'm so fortunate to be surrounded by people who love and support me, even though I spend most of my free time locked away with my laptop. Phil and Taylor, thank you for your unwavering support. I love you both.

Amy, I have to say it again—without you, I would have never written a word. Thank you so much for your patience while reading through this book and for not killing me for changing it a hundred times. I love ya, honey!

My betas Valerie Hayken, D.E. King, Donna Lorson, and Jules from across the pond, and of course Amy for your suggestions and catching the many, many things I missed.

Sheri, my cover artist, who was so very patient with me when I threw this book in her lap at the last minute and begged for a cover. She never fails to impress me.

Kathy Smith, who swears that I am solely responsible for all her gray hairs. She's still a great friend after all I put her through...on purpose.

Last but never least, my dear editor, Tara Young, who has developed an addiction to Excedrin because of me. She swears she still loves me, but I think she may be crafting a voodoo doll in my honor. She was sick and had the misfortune of having a car accident while editing this book. She insists that both were my fault and is demanding a trip to Paris. I'm looking for a second job now so I can afford the airfare.

THE TAKING OF

EDEN

Prologue

Slate blue eyes snapped open at exactly five thirty. After years of repeating the daily process, her body needed no prompting from an alarm to rise at the same hour each morning. She ran her fingers through her shoulder-length brown hair while walking into the bathroom to begin her daily regimen. She stared at her reflection in the mirror while brushing her teeth, frowning when she realized her eyes looked red and puffy. After applying some eye drops, she stepped into the shower, waking fully when lukewarm water hit her in the face.

With her wet hair wrapped in a towel, she walked naked into the kitchen to start a pot of coffee. This morning, she felt self-conscious for the first time. Unable to shake the uneasy feeling that someone was watching her, she pulled the towel from her hair and wrapped it around her body. She glanced around the room as goose bumps rose on her skin from the stranger whose eyes she felt upon her.

She returned to the bathroom to finish getting ready, unable to shake the eerie feeling that someone was there. When she was dressed, she cautiously walked through her house, feeling that at any moment she could come face-to-face with someone. Grabbing her coffee, she hurried to be on her way and free of the creepy sensation that made her skin crawl.

Pausing in the foyer to pick up her purse and keys, she took one last glance in the mirror. Her tailored navy business suit fit her tall, slender form well. The azure blouse brought out the blue in her eyes. Hair, lipstick, and makeup were flawless; she was ready to face the world.

It was when she reached for the door and found that it would not open that the trouble began.

"How long has she been like this?" Jamie Spencer asked, feeling deep sorrow and compassion for the beautiful patient she watched through the observation window.

"Since the day they brought her in, a month and a half ago," Holly Patton sighed. "Each day is the same; she seems to be going through her daily routine of getting dressed for work. When she realizes that she can't open the door, she becomes agitated and sometimes has to be restrained."

"It's so sad," Jamie whispered against the glass. She could never separate her feelings of empathy and compassion for her patients. Facing death and illness that she was powerless to control, she resigned from her job as a neuro ICU nurse and took what she perceived to be a more sedate position at McManus Mental Health Center.

Holly stood just behind Jamie, studying the new nurse's face reflected in the glass. Fine lines around intelligent brown eyes told the truth of her age despite the blonde ponytail that sat high on her head, making her appear much younger. Baggy scrubs hid from view what Holly suspected to be a well-toned body from the muscle displayed in her arms. The senior nurse surmised that Jamie would have no problems handling herself with some of the more unruly patients.

"If you're wealthy or famous in the Carolinas, this is the place to come to get your mind back in the game or to wean yourself off whatever has you by the tail," Holly explained as they continued the tour. "Discretion and privacy is our creed. According to Carmen, our supervisor, that's why you were chosen for this job—aside from the fact that your previous employer sang your praises."

"I respect the privacy of all my patients, so that won't be a problem." Jamie smiled back at Holly, sensing a sudden underlying tension.

"The public as a whole doesn't even know we exist; that's of course why we're tucked away in the woods. There are no advertisements, nor are we listed in the phone book. That's why personnel contacted you; otherwise, you would've never heard of us."

"Then how do you generate business?" Jamie asked as she followed Holly through the maze-like hallways.

"Simply by word of mouth in the most elite circles." Holly stopped and looked around before turning her attention on Jamie. "And be careful what you discuss within these walls, Jamie. You'll find that this place is unlike any other you've ever worked for; covering your ass is a must."

ROBIN ALEXANDER

Chapter One

Dr. Susan Lappin pushed away from her desk and rubbed her fatigued and weary eyes. Today was the day she had set aside to handle the paperwork she dreaded to contend with. She pushed herself hard through the mountain of forms and files because tonight she had a date with a goddess. Her pulse quickened in anticipation. Never in her life had she enjoyed the company of a woman so sexy and alluring; she loved seeing the desire in the eyes of others for what belonged to her now. Glancing down at her watch, she was pleased to note that she had plenty of time to make it home and shower before the goddess was due to arrive.

Susan was not a fool. She had no outstanding physical attributes that would catch the eye of someone like Laura McManus. She wasn't wealthy either—far from it. Her financial situation was the reason she agreed to Laura's little extortion scheme. The only thing the pudgy doctor had going for her was the ability to keep Laura's lover confined while they chipped away at her bank account. That alone would keep the voluptuous blonde in her bed for as long it took to extract the money, then leave everything behind. After that, it didn't matter to her whose bed Laura shared.

Brown eyes watched from a distance as Carmen Hollis led her special patient on a walk around the grounds. When they drew closer, Jamie smiled as Carmen quickly ushered her patient past her, making it painfully obvious that she had no desire to be drawn into a conversation. The patient's slate blue eyes caught hers for a moment as they passed, leaving Jamie to stare after them with a strange sense of foreboding.

The patient Jamie had come to know as Ellen looked back over her shoulder with such a sad expression in her eyes that Jamie felt compelled to run to her, but she fought the urge. She watched helplessly as Carmen tugged her forcefully toward the glass doors of the mental facility. The patient allowed herself to be led but did not release Jamie from her gaze until she disappeared behind the doors.

Sitting in the shade of an oak tree, Jamie nibbled at her lunch and wondered if she had given up too easily on her job at the hospital. This quiet facility in the middle of nowhere was a far cry from the place she came from. Her new job wasn't filled with the challenges that she faced at the busy hospital, but the work still invigorated her. She had developed a fondness for all her patients, and they responded well to her. Jamie's idea of care was to treat the whole patient, not just his or her condition. Her compassion and devotion to their comfort and needs was apparent in all she did. This made her an instant favorite of all in her care, with the exception of one.

Ellen Edmonds was a mystery to her. Often when she had a spare moment or two, she would find herself at the observation window of the mysterious woman's room, mesmerized at the way Ellen paced back and forth like something wild in confinement. Other times, she would appear as though she was diligently working on something, her brow furrowed in deep concentration working with objects that weren't there.

She learned early on that none of the staff had access to Ellen's chart and not to question it. Carmen, the nursing supervisor, was solely responsible for her care and made that fact implicitly clear when Jamie questioned the wisdom of keeping a patient's chart from other caregivers. She argued that if Carmen was off duty and Ellen needed emergency care, they could do more harm not knowing anything about her medical history. Carmen curtly dismissed her claims by stating that she could be reached anytime, day or night, and could be there within five minutes.

"Unorthodox, very unorthodox," Jamie murmured under her breath.

"What's unorthodox?" Holly startled Jamie as she sat across from her at the picnic table.

Jamie regarded Holly as she spread out her lunch. They'd only known each other for a month but clicked instantly. Their friendship had grown close almost overnight, and one often knew what the other was thinking and communicated with a nod or glance.

Holly seemed to share her obsession with the mysterious patient. Jamie found her time and again at the observation window watching Ellen with a grim expression on her face. Jamie debated internally for a moment, choosing her words carefully. "I probably shouldn't say anything. I've only been here a month, and I'm sure it would be considered audacious of me to criticize policy already."

Holly glanced around as she bit into her sandwich. She looked back at Jamie and swallowed the bite before speaking. "You're wondering about Ellen and why all the secrecy. We all do, but everyone here knows not to push Carmen. The last person who did bounced out of here so fast she didn't have time to collect her personal belongings. The doctors don't question her authority, and the administrator thinks the sun rises and sets on her shoulders." Holly took another look over her shoulder, then lowered her voice.

"When Ellen arrived, Carmen called a staff meeting and explained that Dr. Lappin was administering some new medications and the dosing was complicated. Carmen is the only one the doctor trusts with this task. She told us in no uncertain terms that she was her patient and strictly hands-off. Even when the nursing assistants take her to bathe, Carmen oversees the whole thing. And don't even try to talk to her when Carmen isn't here in the evenings because she has little snitches everywhere who want to remain in her good graces."

"I've never worked in a place where patient information is withheld from the staff. Is this standard procedure around here?"

Holly took a sip of her drink and glanced around again, making sure no one was close enough to overhear. "I like you, Jamie, and I think you're an outstanding nurse..." Holly chewed her lip for a moment. "I'm about to tell you something that I don't want repeated. If you break my trust, it could be detrimental to Ellen, and I will straight up kick your ass. Give me your word that this will stay between us."

Jamie stared Holly in the eyes. "You have my word that whatever you say will never be shared with anyone unless we both agree on it."

Satisfied with the response, Holly continued cautiously. "A week before you started here, Carmen got into a car accident on her way to work. No one was injured, but she was significantly delayed getting here. You can set your watch by her; she's never late. This concerned me because I knew that Ellen was due for her meds, so I went to her room and sat with her until Carmen arrived." Holly paused and took a bite of her sandwich, fighting back the grin as she watched Jamie's eyes go round in frustration.

"She was awake when I walked into her room and sitting up in bed. I explained that Carmen would be delayed and asked if she needed anything. She inquired about having a phone put in her room and wanted to know why they were still keeping her here. She seemed to think she was in a hospital, and I thought it wise to allow her to continue to think so."

Holly took another sip of her drink. "Rumor has it that she had a complete breakdown and babbles like an idiot. Carmen describes her as totally incoherent, but the woman I talked to seems..." Holly paused again and looked over her shoulder. "I don't know. It's just strange. You'd have to talk to her yourself to understand."

Jamie rubbed her brow, confused by what Holly was trying to tell her. "I'm not sure what you mean by all of this. It is strange that they keep everyone away from her, and I can't deny that it concerns me, but I don't know what you're implying."

"I've watched her ever since that morning I spoke to her. She seems like a perfectly normal person until she gets her meds, then she whacks out."

"What about her family?" Jamie asked as she tucked her half-eaten sandwich back in its bag. "Surely they can tell us if she's acting normal or not."

"Not a soul has come to visit her since she's been here. Don't you find this strange?"

"Okay, let's cut to the chase here," Jamie huffed in exasperation. "Are you saying that she's being held here and experimented on like a lab rat? That just doesn't make sense, especially for a place that caters to upscale clientele."

"You're right, it doesn't, but I think you should talk to her, and afterward, if you don't agree that something is very suspicious about her, then I'll drop it."

Jamie looked at Holly incredulously. "After what you just told me, you want me to waltz into her room and have a chat? Why don't we just talk to one of the other doctors about this or even Dr. Lappin?"

"I don't think that would be a very good idea. I've never met Dr. Lappin, but I've seen her come in from time to time. Carmen is with her the minute she walks in the door and she doesn't so much as acknowledge the rest of the staff. Whatever is going on, you can bet Dr. Lappin is involved, and if we ask another doctor on staff, she may get wind of it."

Holly watched as Jamie nervously played with her hair. "Listen to my plan before you get all freaked out. Carmen arrives at six on the dot. If you get here around five thirty, you'll have a few minutes to talk to Ellen undisturbed. Everyone is busy with paperwork before shift change and I'll stand lookout. You can get in and out before anyone notices you're even here."

Jamie shook her head nervously. "I just took this job, Holly, I can't afford to get my ass in a sling already."

"Think about it, Jamie. They could be doing something very wrong here, and we can't just turn a blind eye to it," Holly pleaded as she packed up the remainder of her food.

21

"I don't like sticking my nose where it doesn't belong," Jamie mumbled as the internal debate raged inside of her. "What if we're way off base here?"

"There's only one way to know for sure. You have to admit that things simply don't add up."

Jamie exhaled. "Okay, I'll do it, but you have to promise me that you'll be on the lookout. I have no desire to return to the hospital with my tail tucked between my legs after being fired for meddling in someone's private affairs."

Holly genuinely smiled for the first time during their conversation. "I've got your back. Now remember, we don't discuss anything unless it's out here or away from the center altogether. Let's get back in there before Carmen the Terrible hunts us down."

Jamie found it hard to concentrate on her work as the conversation with Holly played over and over in her head. She tapped her pen nervously on the nurse's station desk as her mind wandered. She was brought back to the present when an angry voice called her attention.

"Did you sleep with him, too?" Jamie looked up to find Mrs. Hammond standing in front of her with a look of contempt on her face.

"Excuse me, Mrs. Hammond?"

"You heard what I asked you. Don't play coy with me, you little tramp!"

Jamie glanced at Holly for help. Her friend turned her back to hide her laughter, leaving Jamie to fend for herself.

"What are you talking about, Mrs. Hammond?" she asked with a smile.

"My husband, of course! He's played hide the salami with half the women in this state and is partial to pretty blondes!" The patient spat angrily.

"Mrs. Hammond, I can assure you it has never crossed my mind to be intimate with your husband. I'm a lesbian."

The older woman's face fell slack. "Oh" was the only reply she could muster before one of the aides came to the rescue and

THE TAKING OF EDEN

led the woman back to the commons area where she could watch her favorite television program.

Holly still had her back turned to Jamie, but her body shook with silent laughter. "Bitch," Jamie said, as she threw an unopened pack of peanuts, hitting Holly square in the back. Holly spun around in her chair and chuckled out loud when she realized that the patient could no longer hear them.

"That was priceless!" she said with tears streaming down her face. "I've gotta tell Kelly about this, Mrs. Hammond rips her up daily. Maybe she can claim to be a lesbian, too. That was good, by the way. I've never heard anyone silence that woman so quickly," Holly said as she wiped her eyes.

Jamie crossed her arms and leaned back in her chair. "The only problem with that is that Kelly *is* straight."

The grin dropped from Holly's face. "And you're not?"

It was Jamie's turn to laugh. "Nope."

"Wow…well, I mean it's your…um…thing, I guess," Holly stammered as her face colored.

"Does this offend you?"

"No, not at all. To each her own, ya know? Really, Jamie, it makes no difference to me. I like you for who you are. You just shocked the hell out of me," Holly said as she stood. "It's time to give Mr. Allen his meds, but we'll continue this conversation later. I wanna know all about how two women do it," Holly said with an evil grin as she walked away chuckling.

"Holly?" She paused as Jamie called after her. "You have a great ass."

"Bitch," Holly mouthed at her before disappearing into her patient's room.

Jamie heard a ruckus coming from the south hall. Knowing that was where Ellen's room was located, she ran to see if she could be of assistance. She rounded the corner just in time to see two nursing assistants and Carmen dodge a chair.

"Miss Edmonds, please calm down," one of the assistants pleaded while she ducked as a plate narrowly missed her head.

"How many times do I have to tell you that I am not Miss Edmonds?" The angry patient screamed at the top of her lungs.

23

Jamie watched from the safety of the observation glass. She had only heard of this patient's antics but never had the opportunity to witness it. Normally, she would have stepped in to help, but since Carmen made such a fuss about no one handling Ellen Edmonds but her, Jamie leaned against the wall and watched in fiendish delight.

One of the assistants took a cautious step forward and tried to reason with the patient who was already choosing another weapon from her arsenal. She waved a bowl of something that Jamie could not distinguish at the woman who timidly approached. "Are you hungry?" Ellen asked as she taunted Carmen and her staff. "I'll stuff this down the throat of the first person who gets anywhere near me!"

The assistant stopped dead in her tracks. Carmen stood frozen to the spot, as well, obviously trying to formulate a plan.

"I want a phone, and I want it now!" Ellen seethed as she kept a steady eye on the three women kept at bay with a plastic bowl.

"Miss Edmonds, you need to calm down, we're only trying to help," the other assistant said, trying to draw attention away from Carmen and the other assistant.

"Bitch, you can call me bull corn if you want, but stop calling me Miss Edmonds, that's not my name!" the patient screeched as Carmen and the other woman grabbed her at the same time. They wrestled her to the floor but not before she managed to clock Carmen in the forehead with her bowl, covering her face and shirt with oatmeal.

Jamie watched in dismay as they sedated her. She was really enjoying seeing Carmen, who acted as though she were royalty, get knocked down a few notches. She watched as Ellen's head lolled to the side after a few minutes and the battle was over. Carmen stomped from the room, as the cut along her right eyebrow bled profusely.

Jamie straightened up and looked at her supervisor with mock concern. "Carmen, let me take a look at that for you."

"I'm fine, you need to be tending your patients," she said brusquely as she stormed off.

Jamie watched in amusement as the petite nurse disappeared down the hallway. When Jamie first met Carmen, she considered her attractive, with her long dark hair and brilliant green eyes. Hair and makeup were always flawless, but when she opened her mouth, her condescending air became obvious. Jamie quickly reconsidered her first assessment.

"Hello," the sultry voice purred into the phone.

"Laura, are you still in bed?" Susan asked grumpily, exhausted after only three hours of sleep after the marathon sex they indulged in the night before.

"I was just about to get up, but your bed is very comfortable. You should've slept in," Laura said.

"I have patients to see, and people I owe money to are threatening to break my legs. Sleeping is not an option for me."

Growing impatient with the attitude being projected at her, Laura got to the point. "What is it that you want, Susan?"

"I want to know that you're busy securing my future. I have a lot at stake here, and I want to know that you're handling things!" Susan hissed into the phone. "I've already gotten two calls this morning about my outstanding debts. I don't have to remind you that these people would be just as happy killing me as they would be collecting their money."

"Relax. I'm taking care of things. I can't just transfer the funds in one lump sum. This has to be done carefully. Although, I'm the only one she has given full access to her files. I don't want anything to look too obvious until we're ready to go. You need to learn to trust me, Susan, like you did last night when I tied you to this bed."

Irritable and not in the mood to be toyed with, Susan went for the jugular. "She trusted you, Laura. How do I know you won't turn the tables on me, too?" Susan pushed a little too far, and the dial tone was the response Laura chose to give.

The doctor's attitude reminded Laura of her mother as she rolled over in Susan's bed and cursed them both under her breath. Nothing she ever did satisfied either woman. Her mother continually harped on her to pursue a career or marriage. Her family was filthy rich, why would she need to do either, she thought bitterly. At her mother's behest, her father had stopped the constant money that graced her bank account each month until Laura learned to be responsible.

At first, she blew off the threats of her parents and continued to travel and spend exuberant amounts of her family's fortune on whatever she desired. The day she received the amendment to her father's will leaving her virtually nothing, she got the picture. Like a spoiled child, she began to plot against her own flesh and blood. And with the money she was soon to have in her cold hands, she could simply disappear while her family suffered the consequences of her actions.

Burrowing deeper into the blankets, she thought back on the night she met the doctor. After meeting Susan at a dinner party thrown by her father to celebrate the opening of his fourth mental health facility, Laura did her homework and found that Dr. Lappin was in a world of financial difficulty. Laura was a beautiful woman, and she used her looks and talents to get exactly what she wanted. It wasn't that hard to convince the doctor to take part in the scheme. Money and sex were always persuasive, and the good doctor's drug habit put her at a serious disadvantage.

Had her lover not been such an ass and refused to attend the party, things might not have gone so smoothly. Eden Carlton had no desire to mingle with the social elite who flocked to such functions. This infuriated Laura, which is why, she surmised, she entertained the flirtations of the repugnant doctor. She was nothing like Eden.

At five-foot-nine-inches tall, Laura was the same height as Eden. Their stark contrast made them one of the sexiest couples amongst the people they knew and socialized with. Eden's hair was dark brown and hung just past her shoulders. Laura's was long and blonde. Eden's blue-gray eyes possessed warmth and sincerity, while Laura's nearly black eyes were mysterious and dangerous.

The minute she learned about the elusive Eden Carlton, Laura was obsessed with getting close to the woman. She gained employment at one of the many companies owned by

Carlton Industries, much to the delight of her parents. Through manipulation and deceit, she wormed her way into the inner sanctum of Eden's world.

Eden's grandfather built her a healthy and stable empire. She had no need to be involved with the day-to-day operations of the companies she owned. Instead she kept a small staff of highly trusted people to mind her business, most of whom were well beyond retirement age. It came as a great surprise to all who knew her when she allowed Laura into this group as her personal assistant.

Acquiring the position was easy for Laura, considering what she had to do to get Eden into her bed. She had never met anyone like Eden Carlton. The beautiful brunette could easily have anyone she wanted but chose to be alone. When the relationship intensified in Laura's opinion, she felt sure that Eden would ask her to share her home, but the offer never came. Her lover seemed content to indulge in an occasional dinner or sexual romp, but there was a part of her that no one could touch, not even Laura.

Eden was one of the wealthiest women in the South and a recluse who lived in a modest house just outside of Wilmington, North Carolina. Her only extravagances were her clothes and the SLK30 Mercedes Roadster she loved to drive. The only people she associated with were a handful of friends she had made over the years who were content with occasional contact when Eden felt like initiating it. Every so often, Eden would throw a dinner party, but for the most part, she preferred to be alone. This was her undoing, and Laura took full advantage.

ROBIN ALEXANDER

Chapter Two

Jamie was relieved when she pulled into her parking space and spotted Holly's green Camry already in its spot. She instantly regretted not bringing her jacket when she stepped out into the crisp autumn morning. By the time she met up with her co-conspirator, her teeth were chattering, not so much from the cold, but from the nervousness she fought to suppress.

Holly had already convinced the night nurses to knock off early, leaving her to contend with a couple of aides who were busy preparing for shift change. She and Jamie were alone in the nurse's station, and she whispered into Jamie's ear, "I'll page you if she arrives early, but I'm certain she won't get here till six on the nose. You need to be mindful of the time and be out of there at five till. Remember what we agreed. We don't discuss anything unless we're outside or away from the center." Holly gently pushed Jamie toward Ellen's room.

Jamie was surprised to find the mysterious patient awake and sitting up in bed. She walked timidly into the room, unnerved by the eyes that bored into her. "Good morning, Miss Edmonds. I'm Jamie. I just dropped in to see if there was anything you needed." She winced when she remembered that the woman had adamantly denied that was her name when she bounced a bowl off Carmen's head. Jamie took a quick glance around, making sure there was nothing that could be used as a weapon within the patient's reach.

"You have me confused with someone else, my name is Carlton," the patient responded, obviously annoyed. Jamie wondered for a second if she was going to see the side of Ellen

Edmonds that caused Carmen to have five stitches put into her forehead.

"Carlton is an interesting name for a woman," Jamie replied politely.

"My name is Eden; Carlton is my last name, you twit. How the hell do you people keep up with who you give medications to?"

Jamie ignored the jab. "I'm sorry, Miss...Carlton, I'm still getting used to the early shift. I occasionally forget my own name before I've met my coffee quota for the day. The bright side of all this is that I'm not dispensing meds this morning."

"How long are you people planning to keep me here?"

"To be honest, I'm not sure when the doctor plans to release you."

Eden pawed clumsily at her gown. "I don't see anything wrong and I feel okay. What's the holdup?"

"When your regular nurse gets here, I'm sure she'll be able to answer your questions. Do you mind if I ask you a few? Maybe we can expedite things."

"If it'll get me out of here sooner, I'll answer anything."

"Can you tell me anything about your medical history? Are you on any medications?"

"I had my appendix removed a few years ago," Eden responded groggily as her eyes rolled up into her head momentarily.

"Do you have a regular physician?"

"I was healthy before I got here," Eden snapped.

Jamie bit her bottom lip; this was not going as easily as she hoped it would. "Do you remember the doctor's name who performed your surgery?"

"Something that starts with a B...Biggs, maybe."

"Could it have been Dr. Briggs?"

"Maybe," Eden responded sleepily.

"Do you have any family you would like me to call for you?"

Eden stared off into space for a moment. "I really don't have any family to speak of. Do you have any idea when I'm going to get out of here?"

Jamie ignored the question. "How old are you, Miss Carlton?"

"I'm...I can't remember right now."

"Are you married?"

"Are you about to ask me out?" Eden replied sarcastically.

"No, ma'am, it's just general information for the chart." Jamie smirked back.

"I'm not married, and I'm 33." Eden smiled triumphantly as the tidbit of information returned to her clouded memory. "I'm getting very sleepy again, the medicine you have me taking makes me just want to sleep," she said as her head lolled to the side.

Jamie glanced at her watch. "Miss Carlton, what's the last thing you remember before coming here?"

Eden raised her head from the pillow and blinked at Jamie as she thought. "I remember being at work...having dinner. I'll have to think about that for a while," she said as she fought to keep her eyes open.

"Miss Carlton?" Eden opened one eye and looked at Jamie. "Let's keep this conversation between us; I don't want the other nurse thinking I'm checking up on her work." Eden nodded slightly and was asleep before Jamie made it out of her room.

Jamie arrived back at the nurse's station with time to spare. She and Holly exchanged knowing glances. "Hey, Jamie, do you wanna go have a few beers with me tonight?" Holly called out loudly. "I'm craving that fried cheese they serve at Newman's."

"That sounds wonderful; now I'll spend the whole day craving that damn cheese! We're leaving the minute our shift ends," Jamie called over her shoulder as she began to make her rounds.

Jamie surmised that since she wanted the day to pass quickly, it would drag along one agonizing minute at a time. She had made her rounds and been over her paperwork a dozen times. When her last break came around, she chose to simply wander the halls instead of going outside for a breath of fresh air.

She shuffled along the hallways toward Ellen's room; trying to appear nonchalant, she paused in front of the observation glass. The room was empty, and as she turned to walk away, she ran straight into the woman who dominated her thoughts.

"Oh, excuse me," Jamie said, taking a step back.

Ellen said nothing but simply stared at the blonde nurse who stood in her way. Two nursing assistants stood on either side of her, both with a tight grip on her arms; they looked at Jamie with a peculiar expression.

"I was just taking a walk," Jamie offered by way of explanation.

"Unless there was a schedule change I'm unaware of, you're not at your assigned station," Carmen said brusquely as she approached.

Aggravated with Carmen's tone, Jamie shot back in challenge, "I'm on break and just wanted to stretch my legs." She glanced back at Ellen, who was staring at her with unfocused eyes. Jamie's stomach tightened into knots as she feared that Ellen would say something about their talk earlier that morning.

"Take her back into her room," Carmen ordered the nursing assistants. "I'd like a word with you alone," she said to Jamie as she pulled the door closed behind them.

Sensing a reprimand, Jamie went on the offensive. "When I worked in the hospital, it was not uncommon to walk the halls for a little exercise. Why do I get the impression that's not accepted here?"

"I have no problem with you walking the halls when you're on break. But this is the second time I've found you in front of this particular patient's room. I think I've made it clear that this patient is not like the others and is strictly under my care."

Jamie stepped back as Carmen drew closer. "I have no intention of getting in the way of you treating *your* patient. I was trying to be of help earlier."

Carmen smiled sardonically. "I think your break is about over now. You need to get back to your work station."

Jamie bit her tongue, and without a word, she turned and made her way down the hall, feeling Carmen's glare at her back.

When their shift ended, Holly and Jamie were in a race to get to the bar. Holly gunned the engine of her Toyota as she spun out of the driveway with Jamie right behind her. As they pulled into the parking lot, Holly was the first to leap from her car. "Last one in buys the first round," she taunted. Jamie was closer, but Holly's long legs gave her the advantage, and she grinned mischievously as she pulled the door open just in front of her friend.

They chose a quiet table in the corner where they felt comfortable enough to talk. The pub was already crowded with locals taking their turns at darts. The smell of cigarette smoke filled the air, making Jamie crave her old habit. Patsy Cline played on the jukebox, nearly causing her to forget the stress of the day and the reason they were there.

Jamie watched Holly drum her fingers on the table impatiently. She would not discuss anything serious until the order for the cheese sticks she craved had been placed. Holly's appetite for junk food rivaled her own.

Jamie silently surveyed her co-worker as she told of Mrs. Hammond's attack on Kelly earlier that morning. She admired her big brown eyes with perfect lashes that were naturally beautiful without the aid of mascara. A light spattering of freckles covered Holly's nose and cheeks; coupled with her impish grin, they made her look innocent and in some ways childlike.

Jamie bit back a chuckle when that same sweet face twisted into a scowl as the waitress, who spent way too much time entertaining male customers at another table, casually strolled over to take their order. After the order for beer and cheese sticks was placed, Holly turned and looked at Jamie with a serious expression. "What do you think about Ellen?"

"She says her name isn't Ellen but Eden Carlton. How do we know who she truly is? She may very well be delusional and thinks she's someone else." Jamie took a sip of her beer and sighed as the cool liquid bubbled down her throat.

"Eden Carlton?" Holly's brow furrowed. "Maybe they have her in under a different name for privacy, and that's why they're being so secretive. Maybe she's someone special, although I've never heard of her."

"Do you want my gut reaction?"

Holly nodded, staring at Jamie intently.

"Either she is completely sane or she's on the most mind-bending drugs I've ever seen. Even if she had some sort of meltdown, it doesn't make sense that they keep her locked up the way they do."

"See what I mean? I've never seen them keep anyone so heavily under guard. The only time I see her combative is after Carmen medicates her," Holly said, wincing when she grabbed one of the hot cheese sticks. "And did you notice she wasn't playing around with imaginary things before they doped her up?"

Jamie nodded. "I don't know, Holly, my gut tells me there's something going on here that's not right, but the only way to know for sure is to see her chart."

Holly nibbled a cheese stick deep in thought. "I couldn't live with myself if something happened to that woman and I could've done something about it. We may be off on a wild goose chase, but I truly believe something is going on, if not illegal, then at the very least unethical."

Jamie sipped her beer, enjoying the calming effect it was having on her. "I think I may have a place to start. She told me she had her appendix removed a few years ago. I think I may know the doctor who performed the surgery."

Holly gulped the swallow of beer she had just taken. "Wait a minute. I'm not so sure it's a good idea to tell anyone else about this right now. How well do you know this guy?"

"If it's the man I think it is, I know him very well. He was one of the top surgeons at the hospital where I worked. I looked up to him as a father, as well as a teacher. I can assure you he'll keep this in his strictest confidence."

"You better hope he does because if Carmen finds out we're snooping around, we can look forward to unemployment."

Jamie waved off Holly's attempts to have her consume another round and returned exhausted to her small apartment. It wasn't much, but until she paid off her student loans, it would have to suffice. She stripped out of her scrubs, leaving a trail of clothes on her way to the shower.

She emerged feeling refreshed and ready for bed. She tried to read for a while to help her relax, but the events of the last few days played through her mind like a movie. What would this cost her?

She lay there thinking about her friendship with Holly and how comfortable she felt around her. She'd always been attracted to dark-eyed brunettes. Her friend and co-worker was attractive enough, and she often stole glances at the statuesque woman when she wasn't aware. Still she knew that getting involved with a co-worker was a bad idea, and that was enough to keep her content with just looking. Not to mention the fact that Holly made it blatantly obvious that she was attracted to men.

Her thoughts turned to Ellen Edmonds, as she remembered their encounter earlier in the day. The image of Ellen standing in the hall looking at her with such a hollow expression was so unlike their meeting earlier that morning. Something about the woman haunted her.

Before the end of her shift that same day, she made one more trip down the hall where Ellen's room was located and peeked through the glass. The mysterious patient stood with her back to the observation window, slowly swaying back and forth. Jamie watched her for a while, and as she made a move to leave, Ellen turned slowly and looked at her as though she could see through the one-way glass. Jamie's heart broke as she noticed the tears that streamed down Ellen's face.

The patient approached the glass and pressed her fingertips to it near where Jamie was standing. Overcome with sadness for a woman she did not know, Jamie pressed hers to the glass, as well, feeling as though they shared some sort of connection.

Ellen drew back slowly, lay down in her bed, and curled into a ball.

Jamie dabbed at her own moist eyes, surprised that the incident evoked such emotion within her.

"It's about time you got here!" Susan growled as Laura casually strolled through the door.

She smiled as she set her purse down. "You know, Susan, you have at your fingertips medications that will help you cope with anxiety. You should really try something." Her voice dripped with sarcasm.

"You are my greatest source of stress, my dear," Susan quipped.

"For your information, I've spent the day going over the dummy accounts to assure that the transfers won't raise suspicion, so chill out. I've gone to great lengths to make everyone believe she's on vacation, which is no easy feat when the woman has not missed a day of work in three years. Do you have any idea how many fake emails I have to write each day on her behalf?"

"Dinner is ready. Come sit down." Susan gestured toward the table angrily after being made to wait.

Laura waited as Susan pulled the chair out for her. She smiled, thinking that she had the doctor wrapped around her little finger. "So how is Eden doing? Are you keeping your end of the deal?"

"She is so screwed up that she doesn't even know what day it is. Carmen is taking good care of her."

"In another couple of weeks, we'll put all this behind us and slip away to parts unknown. We'll have enough to live the way we want to in obscurity. Work will become a thing of the past, and debt will no longer haunt you," Laura said smugly, as Susan gently clanked her wine glass with hers.

Laura sipped the wine and grimaced. Susan had no taste for fine wine. Laura already had her replacement waiting in the wings. There would be no place in her life for the doctor; she would make sure Susan would never see a cent of the money she had worked so hard for. Susan wouldn't care; she figured the dead had no concerns anyway, and that's exactly what she would be when the debt collector came calling.

Carmen was startled by the phone ringing, waking her from a deep sleep. She fumbled for the phone and growled when she noticed the time. "Yes?" she answered curtly.

"I'm sorry to wake you, Carmen, but you said to report anything that concerned Ellen Edmonds," the night charge nurse said, feigning sympathy.

Carmen switched on the lamp and squinted as her eyes adjusted to the light. "What has she done now?"

"She requested a glass of water, and when Tom took it to her, she snatched his penlight from his chest pocket and rammed it so far up his nose that he may have to have surgery." The night nurse tried her best not to chuckle as the image of the big man with a light hanging out of his left nostril ran across her mind. "Do you want us to sedate her?"

Carmen felt anger run from the tips of her toes to every strand of hair on her head. "No, don't give her anything. I want you to get some help, and I want her restrained to that bed, and I don't give a rat's ass if her ranting and raving keeps everyone awake until morning!"

The nurse sighed and looked at the others as she hung up the phone. "She wants us to form a posse and tie the little filly down."

"Shit!" was the resounding response from the staff standing around the nurse's station. No one wanted to wrestle with Ellen Edmonds.

Jamie grinned as she pulled into the long driveway of the palatial home of Donald Briggs. In his day, he was considered one of the most gifted surgeons in the country. The aging process had not been kind, and he had been forced to retire when his hands were no longer steady. Nowadays, he spent his leisure time teaching, instead of giving into the lull of retirement.

He greeted Jamie at the door with a warm hug. Just being around the lively young woman who held a special place in his heart made him feel young again. He realized how much he missed the days at the hospital with her.

Jamie watched saddened, as he made his way slowly to the hall closet to collect his coat. She remembered a time when his gait was sure and strong. Even though he was well up in age when she worked with him, he didn't seem old to her. But watching him now, she realized the ravages of time were taking a toll on his body.

She turned teary eyes to the pictures that adorned his foyer, most of which were of his cherished wife, Beth, who had passed away just before he retired. Jamie remembered how Donald seemed to age as he sat at her bedside while cancer claimed her body. He was never the same after her death. And now he spent most of his time alone in the house they used to share, with only memories.

The beautiful autumn day was the perfect complement to lunch at their favorite bistro. Jamie sat back after the meal and breathed in the crisp air as Donald brought her up to date on his life. "I've missed our lunches together." He tenderly placed his hand over Jamie's. "How's your family?"

Jamie smiled at the mention of her loved ones. "Mom and Dad are great and really love living in Seattle. I owe them a visit soon. Ann still lives in Jacksonville with her husband, and my little niece is two years old now and full of mischief like her favorite aunt."

Donald carefully filled his pipe with cherry tobacco, and Jamie closed her eyes for a moment, allowing the aroma to churn up memories of the days they used to spend hours talking. As she looked over at Donald, the smoke swirled around his head before being carried off on the breeze. For a split second, it was just like old times.

"You need to bring her by sometime; I would love to spoil her rotten. It's been so long since I've had a little one around," Donald said with a hint of sadness in his voice.

Jamie's heart sank when she looked into the soft blue eyes peering back at her under white brows. The once-strong hand shook slightly as it clutched the pipe. She fought the lump that rose in her throat as she thought that they might not have many more days like this.

"Well then, it's a date. When I have a weekend off, I'll have Ann bring her up, and we can make a complete brat out of her, then send her back home," Jamie responded shakily, fighting the emotion that coiled up in her throat.

Donald was silent for a moment as he studied the face across from him. "What's troubling you, Jamie? I can tell when something's wrong. It shows in your eyes."

So lost in the moment, Jamie had nearly forgotten the reason she'd come. "Donald, I think I've stumbled onto something, and I'm not sure how to handle it. There's a patient at the center who I think you may have operated on before you retired. I was hoping to dig up a little background information on her."

"Why not have a look at her chart?"

"That's the problem. Her chart is locked in the nursing supervisor's office. It's strictly off-limits. The attending physician will only trust my supervisor with her care."

Donald's brow furrowed. "Why all the secrecy? Is she someone special?"

"I'm afraid I don't know much about her. All our patients are high-profile people, so I'm sure she's someone important."

"And what's this woman's name?" Donald asked as he sipped his tea.

"Ellen Edmonds is what we've been told, but the patient says her name is Eden Carlton."

Donald's eyebrows shot up in mid-sip. He pulled the glass from his mouth quickly and stared at Jamie. "Eden Carlton was one of the last patients I operated on. I remember her well. She drove herself to the hospital with a ruptured appendix. She was in excruciating pain." He set his glass down on the table. "Describe this woman to me."

"She's tall and has brown hair that hangs just past her shoulders, big expressive slate-colored eyes, and very delicate features. She's a beautiful woman."

"Sounds just like Eden," Donald said with a look of concern. "But I don't recall her having any history of mental illness."

Jamie's heart skipped a beat, hoping she was on the right track. "What do you remember about her?"

Donald sat back in his chair and lit his pipe. "I had stopped taking patients and was simply assisting on most surgeries. When she came in, the hospital was extremely busy, so I was forced to perform her surgery.

"I checked on her myself the following day. I thought it odd that no one came to see her; there were no flowers in her room. I questioned her about this as gently as I could, and she explained that she had no family, only an elderly friend who was ill at that time, as well. My heart went out to her, and since I didn't have many patients to tend, I spent a little time with her." He smiled and dipped his white head. "We all need someone when we're sick, you know."

Jamie smiled at her companion. He had been the one to teach her that the patient was a whole person and not to overlook that when tending to his or her illness or injuries. It came as no surprise that the elderly doctor would make time to be of comfort to one of his patients.

"I hated to release her because I knew she had no one at home to help her and she was still weak from the surgery, but she was so determined that arguing was futile. Later that year, the hospital received a healthy donation from Carlton Industries. Eden sent with it a glowing letter singing my praises. I sent her a card thanking her for her kindness, but I never felt like it was enough."

"Donald, I'm afraid that this woman is in trouble, but I can't prove it. I sneaked into her room a couple of days ago and had a short conversation with her. I'm relatively convinced that she would be better off without all the medication they're pumping into her, but I have no way of proving it. Any advice you could give me might make a difference."

"Are you leaving something out here?" Donald asked with his brow arched. "It's not like you to question a doctor's method of treatment."

"I believe they're doing this to her on purpose, rather than negligence. They use the excuse that the meds they're giving her are new and the attending physician will only trust the nursing supervisor with the dosing, but why lock her chart away? We aren't allowed to have any contact with her at all. I know I sound paranoid, but my gut instinct tells me there's more to this, and it's not on the up and up."

"I'll tell you what, write down her doctor's name for me and I'll see what I can come up with. It would be very helpful also if you could find out what they're giving her." Donald smiled and patted Jamie's shoulder.

"If Carmen finds out that I've been snooping, I'll be unemployed."

Donald smiled again. "I'll be very discreet, but if I do uncover something unethical, you may come under fire before this is over."

"I realize that, and I'll cross that bridge when I come to it. I just want to make sure I do the right thing." Jamie paused for a moment, gathering her composure. "Donald...when all of this is over, can we get together like this again? I've missed you."

The following day, Jamie met Holly at what was becoming their second home. Holly had already eaten half of the fried cheese and was enjoying a beer when Jamie arrived. She watched as Jamie dropped into the chair and released a sigh of frustration.

"Why do I get the impression you're going to tell me something I don't want to hear?" Holly said as she set down a half-eaten cheese stick.

"Donald confirmed that he performed the appendectomy on Eden Carlton, and the woman at the facility meets the description of the patient he operated on. How would Ellen know that Eden had that surgery if she was not Eden Carlton herself?"

Holly grinned. "She does have an appendectomy scar. She showed it to me the morning I talked to her, but she didn't say anything about her name being Eden. I think she has so many drugs in her system that she's still under the influence when it's time for her next dose."

"Donald is going to covertly check out Dr. Lappin, but I feel useless sitting around waiting. Holly, I'm considering doing something very unethical. As a matter of fact, downright illegal. I'm not going to ask you to participate, just look the other way for me." Jamie nervously ran her fingers through her hair.

"What are you plotting?" Holly asked, already knowing the answer.

"I'm going to break into Carmen's office and have a look around when I go in for the night shift tomorrow. If that doesn't yield anything, I'm going to draw blood from Eden and have it analyzed."

Holly stared at Jamie in shock for a moment before a grin broke across her face. "Okay, how do we do it?"

"There's no need to risk both of our careers. Let me do this alone, and if I'm arrested, you can bail me out and let me sleep on your sofa till the trial is over and I can move back in with my parents." Jamie grimaced. "I'm not really looking forward to a career as a supermarket checkout girl."

Holly chuckled. "I'm in this just as deep. I hope your parents will take me in, too." She raised her bottle in toast and tapped it against Jamie's. "Tonight we'll consume liquid courage, and tomorrow night, we do the deed."

Al Pittman puffed his cigar as he stared out the window at his prized rose bed and watched the gardener tend his beautiful babies. Soon a heavy frost would come and take them away until the following spring. He wondered if he would live to see them bud again. Truth be known, he was old and tired of being the one to outlive his friends. The only thing that kept him hanging on was his little rose, whom he had not heard from for a while. And he was deeply troubled.

He had grown up with Richard Carlton, and his granddaughter Eden was as precious to him as his own flesh and blood. He solemnly promised the day Richard died that he would watch over the last of the Carltons. He had done an excellent job until recently.

Richard Carlton was not as trusting as his granddaughter, and Al had always been his safeguard. Al worked out of his home and kept a vigilant watch by computer over the day-to-day operations of each company owned by the Carltons. No one knew of his involvement but Richard. Eden was made aware of Al's position within the company just before her grandfather passed away.

Al thought it odd when he read a company email from Eden explaining that she had finally decided to take some time off and venture down to the Caribbean. At first, he was thrilled that the young woman was taking some time for herself, but after nearly three months of silence, he had gone past the point of worry. She had always been a phone call away, and their private email account remained silent.

Before sounding the alarm and calling attention to his presence, he hired an investigator to do some research. When the investigator reported that Eden's credit cards showed no activity, his worry increased considerably. He waited impatiently for news that did not come with every passing day. His precious little rose was missing, and he refused to fear the worst, though it invaded his dreams at night.

Jamie held Holly's hair as she groaned into the toilet bowl. "Why did you let me drink vodka?" She winced in pain as her voice echoed off the inside of the bowl, causing her pounding head to ache more.

"I told you not to drink it, but you forged ahead. Challenging half the bar to a drinking game and picking up the tab was your idea, too."

Holly sat straight up, clutching her spinning head. "You let me do that? How much damage was done to my credit card?"

"Not to worry. The other patrons took pity on you and settled up for their own drinks."

Holly wiped her face with the damp cloth Jamie handed her. "Where's my car?"

"It's still at Newman's. I'll run you by there tomorrow and you can pick it up. Right now you need to get into bed, if you don't think you're going to be sick anymore."

"There's nothing left in my stomach. I think I saw my liver and two ribs in there." Holly pointed at the toilet.

Jamie helped Holly up and guided the staggering woman to her bedroom. She turned her back and gave her inebriated friend privacy while she changed into her sleepwear. "Why don't you stay with me tonight?" Holly asked, as she climbed slowly into bed. "I don't want you out on the road with all the drunks like me at this hour." She groaned as she lay down. "There are some T-shirts in my dresser, help yourself. But you're gonna have to sleep with me. That sofa is not fit to sleep on."

Exhausted, Jamie agreed and grabbed a shirt and slipped into the bathroom, quickly changing her clothes. She gingerly climbed into bed, hoping not to disturb her sick friend, who she presumed was asleep. Lying on her back, she felt her eyelids growing heavy when Holly's voice sliced through the darkness. "What's it like, doing it with a woman?"

Jamie's eyes snapped wide open. "Umm...well, it's different," she stammered nervously.

Holly grinned, hearing the quiver in her friend's voice. "Stop being all timid. Unless you have a dick and a hairy chest, you don't have to worry about me coming on to you."

Jamie released a chuckle mixed with relief. "Thanks, I feel better already."

They both lay in silence, and Jamie's eyes drifted shut once more. She felt sleep begin to wash over her when Holly muttered sleepily, "Although if I were ever going to jump the fence, it would be with you." Jamie's eyes snapped open again in the darkened room. This was going to be a long, sleepless night.

Chapter Three

"Kill that damn cat!" Holly groaned loudly.

Jamie sat straight up in bed and looked around groggily for the offending animal. "What cat?"

Holly smacked her lips for a moment. "The cat that shit in my mouth."

Morning came too soon for the both of them. Jamie fixed Holly breakfast to quell the incessant whining and groaning, after which they picked up Holly's car, and both went back to their own apartments to catch up on some much-needed sleep.

That evening as Jamie pulled into her parking spot at the center, she felt relieved to see Holly's forest green Camry sitting in its place. "Well, Miss Patton, I hope your head is clear now because tonight's the night I become a criminal. Let's just hope it goes smoothly and doesn't cost me my career."

Night shift was considerably more relaxed, especially the early hours of the morning when all the patients were asleep. Most of the staff sat in the lounge and played cards. Holly had bowed out of the game when she lost the last of the cash she had in her purse, assuring the rest of the players she would watch the halls while they carried on.

When she gave the all clear, Jamie began to work on Carmen's office door. She slipped a credit card between the facing and the latch and had the door open in a matter of seconds. She pushed the door open slowly and peeked into the dark office.

She felt strong hands on her back shoving her into the room and stifled a scream as she fell to the floor frozen like a frightened rabbit. The door shut, making the room dark as pitch. "Get up off your ass, we have to find that file!" A familiar voice hissed.

"You're supposed to be my lookout, damn it!" Jamie growled as she ran her hands over the floor trying to find the penlight she dropped when Holly shoved her.

"I told you we're in this together. Besides, they have a hot game of poker going and no one's going to leave that table. Now get up and start looking."

Armed with only penlights, both women searched carefully through cabinets and drawers, finding nothing on Eden Carlton. Holly plopped down in Carmen's chair close to throwing a fit. "Tell me that bitch didn't take that file home with her!" Holly hissed loudly.

"Calm down and lower your voice! Help me think; where else could she have put it?" Jamie whispered, trying to keep her anger at bay.

Holly ran her hands over the calendar that dominated Carmen's desktop. She paused when she felt something tucked under several pages. She pulled out a plain manila folder and examined it. There was no name on the file, but Holly recognized the schedule that Carmen kept immediately.

"Look at this," she whispered as Jamie joined her and peered over her shoulder. A crude handwritten schedule of medications was listed on a single page found in the folder. The handwriting was not Carmen's, but they both knew they had found what they had come for. Holly studied the list intently. "I recognize all these drugs; there's nothing exotic or new here. Although, no physician in her right mind would administer these in such combinations. It's no wonder she becomes combative at times."

Jamie took out a pad and jotted down the list of medications and the dosing schedule. Holly took great care in replacing the file just as she found it. "Let's get out of here. This is making me a nervous wreck," Jamie said as she tugged on Holly's sleeve, pulling her closer to the door. As she reached for the door handle, the door flew open and the room filled with light.

Both women sat nervously fidgeting in front of the nursing supervisor's desk as Carmen made a quick phone call. She never took her eyes from them as she held the revolver in front of her. Jamie's mind raced out of control. She recognized the drugs on the list from her years of working in neuro ICU. Holly was right, no doctor would mix those kinds of drugs unless she wanted to do harm. Jamie came to the quick realization that she was about to be more than fired or arrested.

"Don't you think the gun is a bit much?" Holly sneered when Carmen finished her phone call.

"How am I supposed to know how two drug addicts will respond when caught stealing?" Carmen replied in a cool tone. "I figured something like this would happen, that's why I had the silent alarm installed. I never dreamed that two of my best nurses would stoop to such a level."

"We are not addicts," Jamie shot back. "A simple blood test will prove that we're both clean and that you're lying to cover up what you're doing to one of your patients."

Carmen regarded Jamie with cold eyes. "Your autopsy will confirm your drug use."

In one quick and violent move, Holly stood, grabbing the small table nestled between the two chairs where they sat and slammed it into the side of Carmen's head, sending splatters of crimson across the room. The unconscious form of their supervisor dropped to the floor. Holly checked for a pulse while Jamie sat stunned and unmoving. After making sure Carmen was still breathing, Holly jumped up and pulled Jamie to her feet.

"Listen to me," she nearly screamed as she shook Jamie roughly. "Whoever she called will be here soon, so we have to move fast!" With the front of Jamie's shirt still clutched in her hand, Holly opened the door and peeked into the empty hallway before venturing out. "We need to get Eden and get the hell out of here—now."

Jamie came to her senses as Holly dragged her down the hall to Eden's room. They walked in as calmly as they could and shook the sleeping woman awake. Jamie tried to control the emotion in her voice as she talked to the disoriented patient.

"Eden, we need to leave quickly. Something has gone wrong, and we need to get you out of here. Do you understand?"

Surprised to be addressed by her own name, Eden could only nod and acted obediently when Holly shoved a pair of sweats into her face. "Put these on, it's pretty chilly outside," she said calmly as she tugged at the gown Eden wore.

The decision to take Holly's car was made as they fled the center unnoticed by any of the other staff. The small Toyota would be easier to maneuver than Jamie's SUV. Holly jumped into the driver's seat, and Jamie helped Eden and herself into the back.

Silence filled the vehicle as Holly raced down the deserted tree-lined road. Eden's teeth chattered audibly in the cold car. "You need something on your feet," Jamie said as she pulled off her socks and shoes. "These will help a little," she reassured as she tugged the socks onto Eden's bare feet.

"Do you know a safe place we can go?" Holly asked as she pulled onto the main highway. "We can't go back to either of our apartments, that's the first place they'll look."

"Let's go to the police. We have the proof sitting right here," Jamie said, pulling Eden closer in an attempt to keep her warm.

Holly's brown eyes met Jamie's in the rearview mirror. "Hear me out for a second. There are no real records to prove who has been giving Eden those drugs. They could very easily say it was us. We broke into Carmen's office, Jamie, not to mention how we escaped. We need to make sure we can prove our innocence."

"Are you insane? Carmen had a gun! She wasn't going to let us leave there alive. We need to go to the police before they track us down."

Eden sat straight up, her eyes wide with fear, as she looked down at Jamie's lap. Jamie's eyes followed her gaze, and she gasped to see Carmen's blood splattered across her uniform. "What have you done?" Eden asked in horror.

Jamie reached, trying to calm the trembling woman who recoiled and pressed her body against the door to get away. "Don't touch me, you crazy bitch!" she screeched as Jamie fought to keep her from tugging the handle. "Are you going to kill me, too?" she wailed as she fought against the smaller woman in the backseat.

Holly pulled off the road and climbed nearly into the back as Eden delivered a blow to Jamie's eye, knocking her into the floorboard of the car. Eden was hysterical, thinking she was about to be killed by her kidnappers and fought with all she was worth. Holly drew back and punched her as hard as she could in the jaw, knocking the screaming woman unconscious.

Jamie clutched her eye that had already swollen shut, as she struggled to get up. With her good eye, she could see the blood pouring from Eden's mouth as it flowed freely across the tan leather seat of the car. Holly rubbed her aching hand as she tried her best to formulate a plan.

"Pull the drawstring out of your scrub pants and give it to me," Holly commanded as she did the same to hers. Holly quickly tied Eden's hands behind her back, then carefully tied her ankles together. Jamie watched in bewilderment as she wiped the tears from her injured eye.

Holly jumped back into the driver's seat and pulled the car onto the road. "This way, if she wakes up, she won't beat the shit out of us anymore. Now where can we go? Think of something quick!"

Jamie swallowed hard around the lump in her throat. Her voice was barely a whisper. "I still think we should go to the police."

"Jamie!" Holly shouted. "Look at her! She's tied up and bleeding all over my damn seat! She thinks we kidnapped her. Between her hysterical ass and whoever Carmen is working with, we don't stand a chance. Now start wracking your brain for somewhere we can hide while we sort this out!"

"Donald's...let's go to Donald's house. He'll know what to do. Maybe he'll have something that we can use as proof of our innocence." Jamie winced as the throbbing pain intensified, fueled by the rapid beating of her heart. She never dreamed this would go so badly.

The day was just dawning as they pulled into Donald's driveway. Jamie said a quick prayer of thanks that they had not been stopped by the police on the hour and a half drive to his place. She hated involving Donald, but she had nowhere else to turn. She wondered how he would react to seeing Eden Carlton hogtied in the backseat of Holly's car.

"Pull around back and let me go in first. I want to explain to him what happened so he won't be shocked when he sees her." Jamie opened the door and climbed out of the car, squinting in the morning sun, her eye still throbbing and swollen shut. She hoped that Donald would not have a heart attack when he saw her.

Holly watched as Jamie made her way to the back door of the doctor's home. At any other time, it would have been comical to watch her friend try and walk while holding her pants up. She hoped that they would find some other way to restrain their wild patient, so she could have the drawstring to her scrubs back. She looked into the backseat, relieved to see that Eden was still out cold.

A short while later, Jamie emerged from the house with a bag of ice clutched to her face and Donald close behind her. Donald gave Holly a slight nod, then went straight to the rear of the car to check on Eden. Jamie grabbed Holly by the arm as she got out. "Donald says we're on the news already. They're accusing us of kidnapping. He's got a place where we can stay until he can take care of things for us."

"Maybe you were right. We should've gone straight to the police." Holly rubbed her brow, fighting fatigue.

"It's too late to second-guess ourselves now, sweetie." Jamie sighed as she patted Holly on the back.

It took all three of them to get the tall woman into the house. Jamie cleaned and applied ice to Eden's bruised face as Donald tried to convince Holly to hide her car.

"You can't leave the car here, and you have no time to hide it somewhere else, we have to think of a way to dispose of it."

"So what do you want me to do? Torch it?" Holly answered hotly as she slumped in her seat and rubbed her temples.

"I don't think burning it would be a good idea. That would bring too much attention, and they still might be able to trace it back to you," Jamie offered meekly.

Holly growled. "I was being sarcastic. Can't I just hide it in the woods, you must have miles of land behind this house."

"That's too much of a risk," Donald said firmly. "The incident at the clinic has already been on the news. The police are looking for your vehicle. I think we need to drive it off into the pond. No one would think to look for it there."

"You want me to sink my car in the bottom of your pond?" she shouted, as she jumped up and paced around the kitchen. Donald did his best to convince her it was the wisest thing to do.

"We have no place to safely hide it. The police will no doubt look here since Jamie and I are such good friends. How can I explain away your car?" Donald took a calming breath and softened his tone. "You don't seem to understand what you're up against. Not only do you have the police looking for you, but people who are willing to kill you to keep you silent." Donald paused for a minute, watching Holly absorb what he was trying to explain. "The three of you need to disappear for a little while until I can think of something to prove that you two didn't do what they're claiming."

"And just what are they claiming?" Holly asked as she plopped down into a chair, losing her battle with fatigue and exhaustion.

"Donald said Dr. Lappin was interviewed at the clinic. She claims that Carmen suspected us of drug abuse and asked her advice on how to deal with the matter. She also accused us of having inappropriate relations with Eden and drugging her to hide it, not to mention kidnapping her," Jamie said quietly. "You need to do what he says so we can get out of here."

Holly looked at Jamie, then at Donald. "Where are we going?"

"I have a cabin a few hours from here; you'll be safe there for a while. We have to get rid of your car, though," Donald said, as he pulled his car keys from his pocket.

Holly watched as her car sank into the murky depths of the pond located on the far end of Donald's property. Her heart sank right along with her car as she stood on the bank holding up her pants with one hand and wiping her eyes with the other.

The elderly doctor draped his arm over her shoulders and led her back to his car. "Holly, when this is all over, we'll get you a new car. Right now what's important is that you girls are safe. After this morning, you know what kind of people you're dealing with. The deck is stacked against us right now, so you'll have to lay low for a while."

Eden's eyes fluttered open as she fumbled with the ice pack resting against her jaw. She whimpered as she opened her mouth, causing streaks of pain to shoot through her face. Confusion over unfamiliar surroundings temporarily took her mind off her agony. She jerked her head, causing her to wince when a familiar voice spoke.

"I don't think it's broken, but your jaw is going to be sore for a while. You really should try and keep the ice on it to reduce the swelling."

She blinked a few times as the nurse's face came into focus. Her eye was black and swollen shut. "What happened to your face?" Eden asked, barely recognizing her own voice.

"You happened," the nurse replied tersely. "You freaked out in the car and punched me in the eye."

Eden struggled with the vague recollection of being in the car as she looked around the den. "Where am I?"

"We're at Donald Briggs's house. He's the surgeon who operated on you a few years ago," Jamie said as she gently replaced the ice pack on Eden's cheek.

"Is she awake?" Donald asked as he walked briskly into the room. "We need to get y'all on the road and quickly. We don't have much time. Holly and I have loaded my wife's van up with everything you'll need. I'm going to give Eden something that will help her sleep on the trip and make her more comfortable," he said as her filled a syringe.

Eden's eyes grew wide as she watched him approach.

"I doubt that you remember me, but my name is Donald Briggs, I was your surgeon when your appendix ruptured. I know you're confused and afraid right now, but please believe that these women and I have your best interest at heart."

A vague memory of the man who now stood before her flittered through Eden's mind. She wasn't sure why, but she wanted to believe what he was saying. Even though she had her doubts about the two nurses, she trusted him and surrendered to his care.

Donald watched with tears in his eyes as his beloved wife's van made its way slowly down the driveway. He said a silent prayer that they would make it safely to the cabin before nightfall. He walked back inside his empty house and started a pot of coffee to brew. He would call his brother, whom he knew would be of help, but there would be a lot of explaining to do, and time was of the essence.

"We are in deep shit!" Susan bellowed after she shut the door behind Laura. "How much money have you transferred so far?"

"Not nearly enough, Susan! Don't panic, we just need to make sure that they're never found. You know people who can make this happen."

Susan shoved Laura roughly against the wall. "Did you forget that these are the same people I owe money to? They would rather see me dead!"

Laura wiggled free of Susan's grasp. "I need a little more time to transfer the rest of the money. If they're found, everything will go down the tubes. You've got to figure out a way to make sure they don't turn up before we can get the hell out of here."

Laura poured herself a drink and paced back and forth in deep thought. "Right now we have the upper hand. They can't prove that we were the ones who were drugging Eden. They look like the guilty party. We can still pull this off."

Susan took the glass from Laura and gulped down the scotch, wincing as it burned her throat. "And what happens when we can't explain what Eden was doing there in the first place?"

"You'll come up with something clever," Laura remarked as she grabbed her purse and headed for the door. Susan grabbed her by the arm to stop her before she could reach for the handle.

"Where are you going?" she growled.

"I'm going home. I've got work to do," Laura said as she tried to pull herself from Susan's tight grip.

Susan pulled her close and dug her nails into Laura's upper arm. "You were there when I delivered the blow that silenced Carmen for good. That makes you an accessory to murder. Don't get any ideas about leaving me because I swear I'll do the same to you!"

Laura wrenched her arm free of Susan's grasp. "Be ready to leave when I tell you," she said through clenched teeth as she walked out the door, leaving Susan in her wake.

Susan slammed the door and paced like a wild animal. She picked up the glass that Laura had drank from and slammed it into the wall before going to her safe and pulling out the box that was her true master. Her hands shook as she pulled off her shoe and prepared to inject the one thing between her toes that would calm her.

As the drug entered her blood stream, she relaxed and let the empty syringe fall to the floor. She laughed mirthlessly as the very thing that got her into this mess would bring her peace.

"Am I going the right way?" Holly asked for the twelfth time. "All these roads look the same." She steered the van carefully down the dirt road, doing her best to dodge potholes as she went.

"Just a little farther, according to the directions. Donald was right about this place being remote." She glanced into the backseat at Eden, who was curled into a tight ball and still sound asleep. "I'm amazed she hasn't fallen off the seat yet. She's really out of it."

Just before dusk, Holly pulled the van in front of the small cabin that would be their refuge for an undetermined amount of time. It took both of them to get their patient inside the cabin and onto the sofa. Jamie dropped to the floor after getting Eden settled. "I hope whatever he gave her was enough to keep her down throughout the night. I can't take another ass whipping until I get some sleep."

"Why don't you start dinner, and I'll bring in some firewood so we can take the chill out of this place," Holly said as she helped Jamie to her feet.

"I saw a woodpile out there, why don't you let me help you carry it in, then I can get dinner started," Jamie said as she followed Holly to the door.

"You're afraid she's gonna wake up and dot the other eye, aren't you?" Holly grinned as Jamie popped her in the arm.

"She got in a lucky shot. Remind me to tell you about the time an old woman knocked me out with a can of Ensure. Now that was an ass whipping, but just for that remark, Butch, you can haul the wood in yourself."

Jamie watched as Holly dragged her tired body down the steps in search of firewood. She yawned, thinking it had been over twenty-four hours since either of them had slept. She ran her fingers through her hair and looked around the place they would now call home. Had the circumstances been different, she would have been charmed by the small cabin. The open kitchen faced the living area that contained a sofa and a recliner that looked as if it had seen better days. Just off the den was a tiny bathroom with a shower. Jamie climbed the ladder that led to a loft and noted the most appealing thing was a queen-sized brass bed just waiting to be occupied.

"Very cozy, Donald, you and Beth must've had some wonderful times here," Jamie muttered to herself as she returned to putting away their supplies.

Holly returned shortly after, as Jamie was preparing to make dinner. "Butch is home and she has wood," Holly chirped happily with her accomplishment. She stacked the wood into the small fireplace and found a box of matches on the hearth. "Only one problem here, Butch has never started a fire."

"All right, your butch card has been revoked. It's a good damn thing we aren't roughing it or we would be screwed," Jamie said as she joined Holly at the fireplace and stuffed a paper bag under the logs. "First you have to light something that burns quickly that will set the logs on fire." She demonstrated by lighting the bag and stuffing a piece of cardboard in with it.

"Did either of you morons think to open the flue?" Holly and Jamie turned in surprise to see Eden sitting up on the sofa fanning the smoke.

"For someone who has been rescued, you are one rude bitch," Holly shot back as Jamie pulled the handle to open the forgotten flue.

"Rescued? Is that what you're calling it? How sick do you have to be to take someone from a hospital?"

"Eden, I tried to explain this to you earlier. You were being mistreated at the clinic. We're trying to help you," Jamie said, trying to ease the tension between the two women.

"You both have blood on your clothes. And what clinic are you talking about? I was in the hospital." Eden's body stiffened as Jamie approached her warily.

"Now wait a minute, Eden. Don't start swinging your fists again until you hear me out. You haven't been in your right mind lately; they've pumped a lot of drugs into you. If you'll just listen, I'll tell you all I know."

Holly's laugh was devoid of humor. "I say we tie her ass up again until she calms down and drops the attitude."

"Do you get off on tying helpless people up?" Eden shot back.

"You're hardly helpless, Eden; look at what you did to her eye!" Holly exclaimed as she pointed to Jamie.

"Make the mistake of putting your hands on me, and I'll do the same to you," Eden responded with all the resolve she could muster. She knew she didn't stand a chance against them, and she was bluffing for all she was worth.

"You make the mistake of hitting either one of us again and you'll stay hogtied for a week," Holly said as she prepared to make good on her promise.

"Holly! She's still our patient. Why don't you go start dinner while Eden and I talk?" Fighting the urge to laugh at Holly's loss of temper, Jamie joined Eden on the sofa.

Holly watched Eden closely as she passed her on the way to the kitchen. What she initially thought was anger in her eyes, she now recognized as fear. She immediately felt bad for speaking so harshly. She wasn't sure she would not have reacted worse if she had woken up in the same position.

Jamie chose her words carefully, not wanting to reveal too much too soon. She wondered how much she could explain without telling Eden everything. "Eden, how much do you remember about being at the cli...um, hospital?"

"I remember you waking me up this morning and saying we had to leave."

"You don't remember anything else about being there?" Jamie asked gently, as Holly strained her ears to hear the conversation.

Eden sat quietly for a moment, mentally struggling with fragments of memory. "I don't remember much. What happened to me? Was I in a car accident?"

Jamie shot a quick look at Holly, who remained speechless. "We don't know what happened. We were trying to find out when we were caught. Your records were kept from us; we didn't even know your real name until you told me one morning." Jamie glanced at Holly nervously before continuing. "The drugs they were giving you kind of kept you in la la land. We were hoping you could tell us why you were there in the first place."

The question that Jamie was most afraid to hear came next. Eden looked her directly in the eyes and asked, "How long was I there?"

Jamie looked at Holly for help. She stopped what she was doing and sat on the coffee table facing Eden. "You were there for nearly three months."

Eden's face went blank. Both Holly and Jamie stiffened, unable to determine what was to come next.

Chapter Four

Eden sat silent for such a long time that Holly and Jamie began to fidget and exchange nervous glances. "I thought I had only been there for a few days." Eden's voice drifted off into a whisper. She looked forlorn and bewildered.

Holly gently put her hand on Eden's knee, hoping to be of comfort. "Do you remember anything before you were admitted to the clinic?"

"I'm sorry; I'd just like to sleep now," Eden said as she laid her head on the arm of the sofa.

"We understand." Jamie pulled a blanket from the back of the couch and covered Eden with it. "We're going to make something to eat; I'll wake you when it's ready."

"No, thank you, I'm not hungry," Eden replied, pulling the blanket up against her face.

"Is she asleep?" Holly asked a little later as they sat down to eat.

"I think so; she hasn't moved a muscle, and her eyes are closed."

Holly sighed. "Can you imagine what it would be like to wake up one day and find out that you had been robbed of three months of your life?"

"She must be in shock. I'd probably still be screaming." Jamie took a bite of her sandwich and watched Eden as she slept. "Why would a physician do something like this?"

"They're people, too—good and bad like the rest of us. What I want to know is what happened to land her at the clinic

59

in the first place. Do you suppose she really had a nervous breakdown?"

"We'll know when Donald sorts things out." Jamie set her sandwich down, realizing that she was simply too tired to eat. "I hope she gets her memory back soon or at least some of it. What she remembers will be the key. Hopefully, we'll have some answers when we wean her off the drugs."

"I'll clean this up. Why don't you take a shower?" Holly said as she cleared the table.

"Good idea. I'm gonna go upstairs first; Donald said he and Beth left some clothes here. Maybe they'll have something that'll fit."

Holly made quick work of cleaning the small kitchen and noticed that Jamie had not come back down the ladder. Not wanting to call out to her and wake Eden, she climbed into the loft. Jamie looked as though she had simply fallen across the bed. Holly gently pulled her shoes off and tugged a corner of the comforter over her sleeping friend. She climbed back down the ladder and decided that she was too tired for a shower.

Finding another blanket in the linen closet next to the bathroom, she snuggled into the recliner. She did not want to be far from Eden in case she woke up. Finding five-foot-nine-inches of angry woman standing over her was not something she wanted to wake up to, and she hoped that Eden would sleep through the night.

Jamie felt the warmth of the sun on her face, as it shone through the tiny window in the loft. It took her a moment to realize where she was, and a broad grin broke across her face when she recognized Holly's snoring from downstairs. Wiping the sleep from her eyes, she dug through the small dresser and found some of Beth's old clothes that she hoped would fit.

On her way to the bathroom, her heart nearly stopped when she realized that Eden was not on the couch. The sound of retching drew her to the bathroom. Without bothering to knock, she walked in and found Eden on the floor leaning against the toilet.

Eden looked up at her weakly; her face was pale and sweaty. "I'm so sick," she barely whispered.

Jamie dropped the clothes to the floor and found a washcloth. After wetting it, she gently wiped Eden's face and tried to soothe her as best she could. "Your body has become accustomed to the medication they were giving you. I'm afraid you're going through withdrawals."

Eden groaned. "I feel like I'm dying. I ache all over."

"Let me get Holly, so she can help me get you to the sofa." Jamie pressed the washcloth into Eden's hand and walked briskly from the room.

A moment later, Jamie returned with Holly in tow. The three of them made their way slowly into the living area. Jamie set the bathroom trash can next to the couch and wiped Eden's face and neck with the cool cloth.

Eden's clothes were soaked through with sweat. Jamie did her best to hide her worry. This was just the beginning, and she knew that Eden would be far worse before long.

Holly appeared at her side with a bottle of water. "See if you can take a few sips of this, Eden."

Eden struggled with the bottle, trying to drink as much as she could.

"Not so much, I don't want you to get sick again, just try to take a few sips," Jamie admonished as she gently tugged the bottle back.

"Someone just shoot me and put me out of my misery," Eden said as she pulled her knees to her chest.

Holly smirked and glanced at Jamie, who scowled at the things she knew were going through Holly's head.

"I guess you don't feel much like boxing this morning," Holly teased.

Eden lifted her head from the pillow and glared at Holly. "Eat shit."

The retort froze on Holly's lips as she heard a sound that made her blood run cold. She jumped up and ran to the window.

Jamie heard the sound of leaves crunching under what were obviously tires and the low hum of an engine. "Holly, don't panic, there are bound to be other cabins on this lake. Maybe they're just passing through."

"He's not passing through, he just pulled up in front of the cabin. I don't like this," Holly whispered as she grabbed the poker from the fireplace set.

"What are you going to do with that?" Jamie asked as she grabbed Holly's hand.

"I'm going to beat the shit out of him if he even looks like he's going to come up here," Holly said, wrenching the fireplace tool from Jamie's grasp.

"You're one hostile bitch," Eden said as she watched the two of them struggle.

Holly spun on one heel and waved the poker at Eden. "How would you like me to render you unconscious for a while?"

"Come near me with that thing and I'll ram it up your ass," Eden yelled.

"Stop it!" Jamie said, as she rubbed her temples. "Both of you, settle down. Now is not the time for this!"

The stranger climbed out of the brand new Ford pickup slowly. He walked in front of his vehicle with his hands raised in the air. "My name is Paul," he shouted loudly, hoping that the occupants of the cabin could hear him after he caught a glimpse of Holly watching him through the window. "I'm Donald's brother, and I've brought supplies."

"Oh, thank God," Jamie breathed in relief. "It's okay, Holly. Donald said he was going to have his brother check on us today. See to Eden and I'll let him in."

Jamie walked down the steps and greeted Paul, who was still standing with his arms up. He smiled when she introduced herself.

"I was afraid to knock, I didn't know if you had found Donald's hunting weapons. I'm Paul," he said again as he extended his hand.

Jamie smiled as she took the hand offered her. "It's a pleasure to meet you, Paul. You look like a younger version of your brother," Jamie said as she looked up at the tall man whose dark hair was graying around the temples. His eyes were brown, unlike Donald's, but held the same warmth of the elder Briggs.

"Don't let Donald hear you say that. He still thinks he's a young man. I imagine you have a very sick woman in there," he said, gesturing toward the cabin.

Jamie's expression turned serious. "Yes, she is. I found her a few minutes ago throwing up in the bathroom. Her color isn't good, and I'm worried about dehydration."

"Donald prepared me for that. I've brought some meds that will help while she goes through detox." He dropped the tailgate of the truck and tugged at one of many boxes inside. "Let me get this unloaded, and I'll be able to find the stuff I need to help her."

Jamie grabbed one of the smaller boxes and followed Paul to the cabin. "So you're the other doctor in the family."

"All of the Briggs boys were doctors like our dad. The oldest passed away a few years ago. I'm the baby of the family."

Holly opened the door as they approached and stepped aside to give them room. Paul smiled and set the box on the kitchen table. He dug inside and pulled out a small pouch. "Let me take care of our patient first, then I'll unload the rest of the supplies."

Holly dropped the fireplace tool behind the recliner and smiled sheepishly when Paul looked at her warily.

He glanced at Eden who lay on the couch looking as pale as a sheet. Quickly filling a syringe, he walked over to her and knelt beside the couch. "My name is Dr. Paul Briggs, and I'm going to give you something that'll help with the pain."

Eden was wary of accepting any more drugs after what she had learned the night before, but the pain was too intense to object. She weakly nodded and rolled onto her side, allowing Paul to inject her with the syringe. Pulling a stethoscope and blood pressure cuff out of his bag, Paul checked Eden's vitals. Satisfied with his findings, he whispered a few words of comfort as Eden began to relax and drift off to sleep.

He looked up at Jamie, who was standing over him and watching intently.

"Once we get everything unloaded, I'll go over the dosing schedule with you. She's going to need a lot of attention over the next few days."

Holly cleared her throat, drawing their attention. "I've made some coffee, anybody want some?"

"That sounds wonderful. I was hoping to time my arrival at daybreak. I didn't want to show up here while it was still dark and scare you all to death, so I left the house at three a.m."

"I'm not going to deny that you scared the hell out of us," Holly said as she unpacked the box of food. "I almost worked you over with a fireplace poker."

Paul chuckled. "That might've been just the thing for the crick in my neck. I feel like I've been driving for days."

"Then the least we can do is fix you breakfast and a cup of coffee. I've unloaded the truck and put the boxes on the porch," Holly said with a grin at Paul's surprised expression.

"Thank you. I certainly didn't expect you to unload the whole truck," he said with a smile. "I've brought you plenty of food, and Donald suggested that I pick you up some clothes and personal items." Paul's face reddened as he remembered the debate over tampons versus pads.

Paul cleared his throat. "Um...Donald gave me a general idea about your sizes...there's some underwear in there, too. I'm sure it's not what you're accustomed to wearing, but I did the best I could."

"That's good news. I can't wait to shower and change into something clean," Jamie said with a grin, looking forward to getting out of her dirty work clothes. "I'll settle for clean undies, even if they're granny panties."

"I'll make breakfast since it's the one thing I can cook while you take a shower. It should be done by the time you get out," Holly said as she pulled one of the ice chests that Paul had brought and began to unload it into the fridge.

"Thanks, Butch, I'll be right out," Jamie called over her shoulder as she took the box of toiletries and clothes into the bathroom.

Paul looked at Holly curiously. "She likes to call me that because she thinks it pisses me off," Holly explained with a grin. "I'm not gay, in case you're wondering," Holly said with a wink and watched with satisfaction as Paul's face colored.

"It's good that you two can keep your sense of humor at a time like this, it helps with the stress," Paul said as he began to empty a box into the pantry.

"Picking and arguing with her is the only thing keeping me sane at the moment. This all seems like a dream. Yesterday a woman I've worked with for a long time pointed a gun at me. Today I'm a kidnapper and a fugitive hiding for my life."

"What you've done is a very admirable thing, Holly, though I'm sure you never dreamed it would turn out this way."

"Now that I think about it, we could've done this so many different ways. We should've given Donald more time to see what he could turn up before we broke into Carmen's office. I've always heard that things happen for a reason. Maybe what we did was right." Holly sighed. "I hope we live long enough to know for sure."

"Hopefully, when we purge the drugs out of Eden's system, she can give us information that'll help. Right now our first priority is to make sure she's healthy and you all remain safe and tucked away until we can clear things up." Paul smiled reassuringly and patted Holly on the shoulder.

"Thank you for everything, Paul. Just knowing that you and Donald are looking out for us is comforting."

Holly put on an impressive morning spread of eggs, toast, and bacon. Jamie joined her and Paul at the table. "After we eat, we need to wake Eden and try to get her to eat something. It's not good for her to go so long without food," Jamie said as she gulped her coffee.

"Before we wake her up, there are some things I want to discuss with you both," Paul said, drawing their attention. "The pouch with the medications for Eden needs to be put in a safe place and kept out of her sight. She'll often be miserable as you wean her off the drugs. No matter how much she begs, do not give her more than the dosing schedule dictates."

Paul reached into one of the boxes and produced something wrapped in a towel. "This needs to be hidden in a safe place, as well, preferably not in the same place as the drugs." He carefully unwrapped a revolver and set it gently on the table next to his plate. "Donald has a collection of hunting rifles and shotguns here, but I wanted you to have something small and easy to handle. Do either of you know how to shoot a handgun?"

"My dad taught me how to use one when I was younger. I'm pretty sure I could use it if I had to." Jamie shuddered. "I hope it never comes to that."

Paul slid the gun in front of Jamie. "Good, then you'll be in charge of this. I picked up a pay-as-you-go mobile phone and bought some extra phone cards. It's already been activated and programmed with my phone numbers. Use this only in a dire emergency. Don't call anyone on it but me.

"I've brought enough supplies to last you for a week. If there's anything you can think of that you may want or need, just jot it down before I leave, and I'll bring it out next week. Until then, y'all are pretty much on your own out here, so be very careful."

Jamie stood and fixed a small plate. "I'm going to see if I can get Eden to eat something before this gets cold." The reality of just how dangerous the situation they were in came crashing down on her, and she needed to busy herself before her emotions took control. Holly continued to talk with Paul as Jamie approached her sleeping patient.

"Eden, it's time to eat," Jamie said as she gently shook her. Eden looked up at her groggily, then looked around at her surroundings, seemingly confused.

"I'm not hungry," she said as she yawned and laid her head back on the pillow.

"You need to eat something. It'll help keep your strength up and probably help with some of the nausea." Jamie sat on the couch next to Eden and prepared to feed her.

"I hate eggs," Eden said disgustedly and turned her face away.

"Then eat the toast."

"Perhaps you have a hearing problem. I'm not hungry."

"My hearing is fine, but maybe I didn't make myself clear. You are going to eat this toast and bacon right now." She raised one eyebrow but not her voice. The exchange was so quiet that neither Holly nor Paul was aware of the standoff.

Eden took a piece of toast off the plate and bit into it with her eyes locked on Jamie's. "So, little girl, do you get off on bossing people around?"

Jamie rolled her eyes, her patience waning with the obstinate woman she had risked it all for. "If it gets you to eat, then it gets me off."

Eden cocked her own brow. "Kinky."

"Sleeping Beauty has awakened." Holly grinned as she offered Eden a cup of coffee. "Don't even think about throwing this at me, princess."

"I never waste good coffee," Eden responded as she eagerly took the cup.

"I noticed that you were a little low on firewood outside. I'm going to split a few logs before I get back on the road. I need to do something to work off breakfast anyway," Paul said cheerfully, leaving the two nurses to contend with their testy patient.

Jamie stood and gave Holly a little shove toward Eden, as she stretched her legs. Holly seemed to be in more of an amiable mood, and Jamie decided she would be better at getting Eden to eat.

"You look better now than you did this morning. How do you feel?" Holly asked as she took a seat on the couch.

"Peachy," Eden shot back.

Holly gnawed her bottom lip and glanced at Jamie, who was glaring at Eden. "Look, I know you want to go home; we would really rather be at our homes, too. But until this is resolved, we have to make the best of it. Jamie and I just want to take care of you and get you back on your feet."

"Fine then, just let me sleep. I've eaten my breakfast like a good little girl, now is everyone happy?" Eden replied sarcastically while looking at Jamie.

Jamie exhaled loudly, her frustration apparent.

"Well then, I'm just going to go take a shower and you just relax." Holly smiled at Jamie, who scowled, knowing she would have to stay with Eden while Holly bathed.

Jamie plopped down in the recliner and stared at Eden as she lay back down on the couch. "Are you just gonna sit there and stare at me while I sleep? I can't be that interesting," Eden quipped.

"No, I'm going to wait for you to fall asleep, then I'm going to draw all over your face with a marker," Jamie responded dryly.

"I'll take my chances," Eden said as she snuggled into the blanket. After a minute or two, she opened her eyes and found Jamie still staring.

Jamie smiled, knowing it was irritating the woman across from her. She watched as Eden slowly closed her eyes again. Maybe it was just stress, but Eden's attitude had gotten under her skin. She was accustomed to dealing with difficult patients, but she expected Eden to at least be grateful that they had risked their careers and lives to help her. She grabbed the handle of the recliner and lifted the foot rest, which made a loud pop.

Eden opened her eyes again to find Jamie still staring at her. "You're really beginning to get on my nerves," the sleepy woman growled.

"Good, then we're even," Jamie shot back as she arched her eyebrow. Eden flipped over with her back to Jamie and drifted off to sleep.

Holly emerged from the bathroom shortly after. "Is Paul still chopping wood?" she whispered.

Jamie made no attempt to lower her voice and smiled when Eden raised her head again. "Yeah, and if you don't mind, I'd like to take a walk and get a breath of fresh air," Jamie said, clanging the recliner loudly as she got up.

Holly gently tugged her arm. "Are you okay?"

Jamie ran her fingers through her long blonde hair. "I'm just a little antsy. I think I need a change of scenery."

"Go explore the outdoors for a little while. I'll watch the princess. Maybe she'll do us a favor and sleep till dinner."

Eden granted the favor and slept well through the afternoon. Paul left shortly after lunch, leaving Holly and Jamie to explore their surroundings. Holly was more than pleased when she found that the armoire sitting in the living area contained a television complete with satellite dish. "I hope Donald sprung for the movie package," she said while fishing around for the remote. Her heart sank when the TV screen failed to show a picture. The dish had long been disconnected.

Jamie tended the stew that she had set to cook just after lunch and chuckled to herself when Holly let loose a tide of expletives as she realized their only entertainment would be a sparse pile of VCR tapes.

"That satellite dish on the side of the house is just a big tease," Holly spat as she dug through the tapes. "So far, I've only found some old westerns and two horror movies. There better be popcorn, damn it!"

Jamie set the table and served the stew. "Let's eat first, then we'll wrestle with Miss Personality. She needs to eat and bathe."

"I can't help but notice that you haven't succumbed to the charms of our lovely patient," Holly teased as she tasted the stew.

"I guess I just expected her to be a little different. You know...grateful."

"I know what you mean. I wanted to beat her ass last night and this morning, but after finally getting some rest, I'm finding it easier to cope. She's still got a lot of drugs in her body, and she's just beginning to detox. Things are going to get a lot worse in the next few days. Afterward maybe we'll find a pleasant person. If not, I say we tie and gag her until we can leave here."

Jamie chuckled. "I guess you're right. I'm not sure how I would react to having three months of my life stolen. It wouldn't be pleasant, that's for sure."

Eden stirred and groaned as her caregivers were finishing dinner. "How about a drink of water?" Holly asked as she pressed her hand to Eden's sweaty face.

"Yes…please," Eden groaned. "I feel like I've been run over by a train."

Holly helped Eden sit up and watched as her hands clutched the glass shakily. "I'm sorry, honey, but you're going to have to tough it out for a little while. You've got about two hours before your next dose."

Eden groaned and fell back onto her pillow. "Can't you give it to me early? I feel like I've been beaten." She shot a look at Jamie, who smiled sweetly.

"Try and eat something. Maybe that'll make you feel a little better," Jamie said as she sat on the coffee table and prepared to argue with her difficult patient. She expected more sharp comments, but she was surprised when Eden nodded her consent.

Jamie and Holly watched sadly as Eden's hands shook too violently to hold the bowl, much less feed herself. Holly gently took the bowl from her and began to feed Eden, who looked at her gratefully. "What is hurting you the most right now?" Jamie asked, wanting to help.

"My legs feel like I have Charlie horses in both calves."

Jamie went to the foot of the couch and raised the blankets. She ran her hands up the legs of Eden's sweatpants and massaged the muscles that felt impossibly tight under her touch. "Eden, you need to shave, honey," Jamie said with a giggle.

"I need to bathe. I feel nasty, and I've been wearing the same clothes for two days."

Jamie could feel the tension in the muscles relax as she massaged Eden's legs. She winced inwardly, regretting how irritated she had gotten with her earlier that morning. Eden was obviously in a great deal of pain, and Jamie knew, or at least hoped, that was the reason for her cross behavior.

"After you finish eating, we'll help you into the bathroom. There's no tub, so you'll have to take a shower. Do you think you're strong enough to stand?" Holly asked as she raised the last of the stew to Eden's lips.

"I'd like to try. It would be nice to wear clean clothes again," Eden said as she tried to sit up. "Right now I'd really like to go to the bathroom."

Holly and Jamie helped Eden to her feet and slowly led her on shaky legs to the bathroom. "I can go potty by myself, ladies." She smiled sheepishly as she closed the door in their faces.

"We'll be right outside the door if you need help," Holly called out, as Jamie looked at her in amusement.

A few minutes later, the door opened and Eden stood holding on to the door facing. Her upper lip was already beaded with sweat from the short walk. "Why am I so weak?"

"You're not going to be able to stand for any length of time in the shower," Jamie said as she draped Eden's arm over her shoulder and led her back to the couch, with Holly at her other side. "You're being slowly weaned off a lot of drugs. It makes you ache and feel puny. Looks like you have a sponge bath in your future."

Eden collapsed on the couch. "Oh, boy, that sounds humiliating. I can hardly wait," she said with a growl.

ROBIN ALEXANDER

Chapter Five

"You're not leaving me alone to do this myself!" Jamie hissed under her breath.

Holly couldn't help but chuckle at the shade of red her friend's face had turned. "It doesn't take two people to give a sponge bath. Besides, you're the lesbian; it should be easy for you to touch another woman like that. I'm sure you've had tons of experience."

"This is not some other woman. This is a patient," Jamie growled as she pulled a washcloth and towel from the cabinet.

"Precisely, this is why you should have no problem doing it." Holly pulled out a disposable razor and laid it on top of the towel. "Try not to cut her." Holly quickly walked out of the bathroom and announced that Jamie would be giving the sponge bath and that she would go outside to allow Eden her privacy. Jamie stood in the bathroom and nearly bit through her lip to keep from cursing Holly at the top of her lungs.

Jamie took a deep breath, steeled her nerves, and walked into the room, trying her best to appear nonchalant. Eden's obvious discomfort was written on her face. "Look, I think I can do this on my own," she said nervously as Jamie set the things she collected from the bathroom on the coffee table.

"I'm sure you would be more comfortable doing it yourself, although you're going to need my help with some of it. Give me a few minutes to get the water, and we'll get you all cleaned up," Jamie said brightly as she went to the kitchen for something large to put water in. "Why don't you get undressed and cover yourself with the sheet while I do this?" She called over her shoulder, as her stomach tied in knots. This was a little too intimate for her liking.

She was pleased when she found a large pot and a couple of other dishes that would be suitable for what she had in mind. When they were filled with warm water, she returned to the sofa and could not suppress the giggle that welled up inside of her.

"Go ahead and laugh!" Eden barked out. "I'm pathetic!" The angry voice came from behind the red sweatshirt she was tangled in. "I don't even have the strength to take my own damn clothes off!"

Jamie set the pot down and gave the shirt a tug. The smile dropped from her face when she noticed the tears of frustration threatening to tumble from Eden's eyes. Eden looked away quickly, hating the pity she saw directed at her. She pulled the sheet up to cover her exposed skin, feeling more embarrassed and vulnerable than she ever had.

Jamie quickly retrieved the rest of the pots from the kitchen and set them on the table next to her. "I've got an idea that I think will keep us from soaking the whole cabin. First we'll wash your hair. You can just lie across the couch and lean your head over this." Jamie positioned the pot close by. "I'll pour the water over your hair, then lather you up and rinse. Does this sound okay with you?"

Eden took a deep breath and slid her body down the couch, then leaned her head off the side. Jamie supported her head with one hand and poured the water through Eden's hair until it was saturated. She shifted Eden's head slightly until it rested on her knee, and she began to massage shampoo into her hair. Eden closed her eyes as Jamie worked her hair into a lather. Tense muscles began to relax in her face. Jamie spent a while longer than she normally would have, studying the features of her obnoxious, but beautiful patient.

"How did you get the scar on your forehead?" she asked softly, breaking the silence.

Eden opened her eyes for a moment and looked into Jamie's, and a slight smile graced her face. "When I was a little girl, my grandfather was trying to teach me how to ride my bike without training wheels. He would give me a shove and I would peddle until I lost momentum. Then he would give me another shove. I was so absorbed in what I was doing that I didn't notice the tree branch in my path." She chuckled softly. "I got seven stitches and a huge bowl of ice cream."

"See, your memory is improving already," Jamie encouraged.

"I can remember some things, but I still can't remember what happened prior to being admitted to the hospital."

Jamie's hands paused for a minute. "You weren't in a hospital, Eden; you were in the McManus Mental Health Clinic." Jamie questioned the wisdom of revealing this tidbit of information when Eden's eyes widened and looked into hers. She hoped the revelation would help jog Eden's memory.

"What...did you say? McManus?" Eden's brow furrowed in confusion. Jamie could see the wheels turning behind Eden's stormy eyes.

"Does that mean anything to you?" Jamie asked excitedly.

Eden remained quiet for a minute. "No, nothing. I was just surprised it was a mental health clinic," she answered quietly.

Jamie continued massaging Eden's scalp. "It's okay, you'll begin to remember more as the fog in your head clears."

"My legs are hurting again, and I'm feeling queasy."

"You have an hour or two till your next dose, I'm afraid. After we finish your bath, I'll rub your legs again. Of course you'll have to shave them first." Jamie grinned, trying to lighten the moment.

Jamie carefully rinsed the shampoo from Eden's hair, then applied conditioner as Eden lay patiently with her head on her knee. Once she had Eden's hair wrapped in a towel, she refilled the pots with clean water. "I'll give you your privacy while you bathe. If you need me, I'll be right here in the kitchen."

Eden did her best to clean her body despite the cramps that had begun to intensify in her stomach and legs. Exhausted, she fell back onto the couch and sighed in frustration. "I can't shave my legs; I just don't have the energy."

"I'd be happy to do it for you, if you're not afraid of me cutting you," Jamie replied shyly.

"It doesn't matter if you cut me; my legs are hurting too bad already."

Jamie sat timidly on the end of the sofa. "Why don't you pull the sheet up your legs, and when I'm finished here, we can get you dressed in some fresh clothes?"

Eden pulled the sheet up high enough to reveal her bare thighs. Jamie did her best not to appear nervous, but her hands shook slightly as she spread the shaving cream up and down the long leg presented to her. "I'll tend my bikini line when I'm well enough," Eden said with a smirk, making Jamie laugh.

Jamie gently ran the razor over Eden's legs, hoping that she wouldn't draw blood. Eden lay back watching her. "Do you do this for all your patients?"

"If they need me to, although I don't think I've ever had such a high-maintenance patient before." Jamie smirked back.

"Why did you choose to help me?"

Jamie paused and met Eden's eyes for a moment. "Something wasn't right. The way everything was kept secret wasn't normal, so I began asking questions, only to be shot down each time. Holly noticed it, too, and she confided all her suspicions in me. That morning I talked to you in your room, I knew something was very wrong."

"I remember bits and pieces about coming here, but I don't remember talking to you before." Eden averted her eyes. "What was I like?"

Jamie chuckled. "You were...very interesting. You gave the staff hell whenever you had half a chance."

"I'm not crazy, and I didn't belong in that place."

The smile faded from Jamie's face. "I believe you, that's why we did what we did."

"You risked your life and job for a total stranger?" Eden asked.

"At the time, it didn't seem like that, but when everything began to fall apart, I guess that's what we did." Jamie sighed as she spread the shaving cream up and down Eden's other leg.

Happy to be outside of the confines of the small cabin and alone, Holly walked along the gravel road that circled the lake.

She breathed in the fresh night air, feeling it clear her head. She felt a little guilty for leaving Jamie alone to tend their patient, but she knew if she didn't get away, she would explode and say things she didn't mean. She wondered if life would ever be normal again as she made her way slowly back to the cabin. She smiled to herself ruefully. No, it wouldn't.

Jamie's hand shook as she pushed away from the table. "I can't take this, Holly! Can't we just do it thirty minutes early?" she asked as she ran her fingers shakily through her hair.

Eden shrieked again at the top of her lungs, "You evil bitches!"

"No, we can't give it to her now. We have to stick to the dosing schedule. We can't make exceptions if we want her to get better," Holly stated resolutely.

Eden lay across the couch kicking and pulling at her clothes with all the energy she could muster. Jamie tried to soothe her by rubbing her cramping legs and found herself nearly kicked across the room.

"I know it's for her own good, but she's hurting. I can't take it," Jamie said as she paced back and forth.

"Go outside and get some fresh air. When it's time to give her the injection, I'll call you back in. Take a break." Holly rubbed Jamie's shoulders.

Jamie headed for the door, and the last of her resolve nearly crumbled when Eden pleaded for her not to leave. Holly gave a little nudge toward the door and approached Eden warily.

"Eden, don't even think about trying to hit or kick me. I'm trying to help you. You've got to try and focus on something else besides the pain," Holly said as she sat on the recliner.

Eden's hair clung to her face in a mixture of sweat and tears. Her breath came in pants as she dug her nails into the sofa cushion. "Focus? Focus on what? You hateful whore! You're doing this on purpose!" Eden spat as she doubled over when the spasms in her stomach intensified. "I hate you." She broke into tears again as she buried her face into her pillow.

Holly watched the clock, willing the hands to move faster, as Eden continued to thrash around and curse her, her family, and even her pets. She watched helplessly as Eden's body contorted in pain.

When the time came, she jumped up and called for Jamie, who occupied Eden while Holly retrieved the medications from their hiding place. Her hand shook as she drew the liquid into the syringe. She had wanted to give it to Eden early just as badly as Jamie but knew one of them had to stay in control.

Eden lay as still as she could, though her body trembled, as Holly gave her the injection. Jamie held her and rocked her like a child until she cried herself to sleep. Finding herself even more exhausted from the ordeal, Jamie gave into sleep, as well, and let her head fall back onto the couch in slumber, still clutching Eden to her tightly.

Holly watched them both as they rested. She had so much invested in this, she wondered if she had made the right decision. Would Eden ever be normal again? Was she ever normal in the first place?

Al Pittman paced back and forth, clutching his favorite pipe to his chest. He'd called earlier in the day posing as a family friend and was told by Eden's assistant that she had checked in frequently and had been enjoying herself in the Bahamas. He prayed that it was the truth, but he knew in his heart that something was indeed very wrong.

He knew the assistant was lying; there was no way Eden would stay away for so long without contacting him. He snatched up the phone and made a call. It was time to pull some strings.

"Jamie." Holly shook her friend gently. "Honey, wake up." Jamie opened her eyes slowly and looked up at Holly. "You go upstairs and sleep in the bed. I'll stay down here with Eden."

Jamie looked around disoriented. Holly had already cleaned the kitchen and dressed for bed. "No, you take the bed tonight. I had it last night, that's only fair. Besides, I'd just feel better being close to her."

Holly looked at her friend strangely. "Are you getting a little attached?" she asked with a grin.

Jamie scowled. "No, I would just feel better being down here in case she needs anything. I had a good night's sleep last night, you deserve one tonight."

"Just yell if you need me," Holly said as she headed for the loft, looking forward to sleeping in a real bed after spending the night before in the recliner.

Jamie scooted from underneath Eden and laid her head gently on her pillow. She stood and stretched her screaming muscles. Finding a blanket and pillow, she burrowed into the old chair and lay facing the woman who was still such a mystery to her. She listened to the slow steady breathing and studied the soft features that were not obscured by hair that clung to her beautiful face.

She wondered what kind of clothes Eden usually wore. Did she wear makeup? She certainly didn't need it. Even in her current unkempt state, she was beautiful. "Who are you, Eden Carlton?" she asked quietly in the darkness.

Eden was clad only in one of Donald's old T-shirts and a pair of the new underwear that Paul picked up with the supplies. Jamie smirked, feeling certain that Eden would have never chosen granny panties for herself. Eden stretched and put one of her arms behind her head, causing the shirt to rise a little and reveal her stomach.

Jamie tried to pull her eyes away from the silky-looking skin but was captivated by the sight. Her eyes slowly drifted up the long slender body to her breasts where her nipples strained against the worn cloth. Jamie forced herself to look away, feeling guilty for the thoughts she was having.

She burrowed farther into the chair and found herself staring at a pair of long legs that looked golden in the firelight. She remembered the feelings it conjured when she held them as she ran the razor over Eden's skin.

Jamie's eyes closed, and those same legs were waiting for her in her dreams, only this time, they felt different as she trailed her fingertips up silky thighs.

Jamie was summoned from the land of dreams by the smell of bacon frying. She grinned before she ever opened her eyes, thankful for Holly's consideration. She stretched and groaned, surprised at how good she felt after sleeping in the recliner. She glanced over at Eden who was still sound asleep, one arm hanging off the side of the couch and the blankets on the floor.

After a quick trip to the bathroom, Jamie followed her nose to the coffeepot and poured herself a cup, nearly purring as she took her first sip. Holly glanced over and greeted her with a smile. "Biscuits will be ready soon," she said as she took the scrambled eggs from the heat. "How'd you sleep?"

"Good," Jamie responded cheerfully. "Looks like Eden had a restless night, though."

"That couch can't be very comfortable, and she has been on it since we arrived. I'm not even going to try and get her up into that loft, though." Holly pulled the biscuits from the oven and set them on the table. "I'll fix our plates if you'll see if you can get Sleeping Beauty to join us."

After a tug of war with the sheet, Eden reluctantly got up from the couch with Jamie's assistance. She sat at the table and gulped the glass of water Jamie set in front of her. "Easy there, Spike," Holly said teasingly. "Don't drink so fast. It might make you sick."

"What did you call me?" Eden asked hoarsely.

"Spike, because most of your hair is standing straight up," Holly kidded as she took her seat at the table.

Jamie chuckled.

"What are you laughing at?" Eden asked as she reached again for the water.

"You know what a cowlick is, right? Well, it looks like a whole herd of cows got a hold of your head last night."

Holly and Jamie burst into a fit of laughter, as Eden looked at them with a small grin tugging at the corners of her mouth. "Go ahead, you two, make fun of me while I'm down, some bedside manner you have," she said as she began to chuckle, as well.

"You seem to be feeling much better this morning," Jamie said as she patted Eden on the hand.

"I still feel like I have a terrible hangover, but I'm not aching as bad..." Eden paused for a moment. "I'm sorry about the things I said last night."

Holly smiled. "Don't be. If I were in your shoes, I would've probably said much worse. And it's not over yet, you still have a while to go. The doses will come further apart now, and you'll hurt for a little while, but we'll do what we can to ease your suffering."

Jamie sat quietly, watching the interaction between the two. They both were trying their best to be cordial, but she could plainly see neither seemed to like the other very much. She wondered if Holly was regretting ever getting involved with Eden, who seemed to try her best to be difficult when it came to her.

Chapter Six

"How long is it going to take?" Jamie asked as she paced back and forth through the kitchen.

Paul scrubbed his face with his hands. Still tired from the drive, he was not ready for the onslaught of questions that greeted him when he arrived. "You both know how complicated this is, you've got to be patient."

Holly held up her hand to silence the tirade that she knew Jamie was about to embark on. "Paul, we feel cut off out here. We have so much time on our hands that we do nothing but mull over our predicament."

"Donald has been discreetly digging up the dirt on Dr. Lappin. We still don't have all the pieces of the puzzle, but we're getting close," Paul stated emphatically. "Neither of us want to take any chances with your safety, but we feel this is the best course of action for now."

"What have you found out so far?" Jamie asked before Holly could.

"Dr. Lappin is in major financial trouble, and apparently, the people she owes are not your typical savings and loan organization. She's involved with some very dangerous people. She's also in the hot seat right now because there are no admission records on Ellen Edmonds, there's nothing in the system. Of course, Susan is blaming that on the head nurse Carmen."

Jamie glanced at Holly nervously. "Maybe we should reconsider and just go to the police and take our chances."

"That's not a good idea at this point. Dr. Lappin is one cool customer. They've played the interview with her on the news repeatedly. She has knitted together a very convincing story against you two," Paul said as he sipped his coffee.

"What is she saying about us now, aside from us being drug addicts and molesting our patients?" Jamie asked.

Paul looked up from his cup of coffee. "So you've been watching the news?"

"The satellite isn't hooked up. We've been watching spaghetti westerns all week," Holly growled. "Donald told us about the accusations the morning we left the clinic. Smug bitch, they didn't even write Eden's name on the dosing schedule. We have no way of proving that it was Lappin that ordered the meds."

Jamie felt rage tingling at her scalp.

Paul sighed. "That head nurse would've been the key. If she could've been pressured to tell the truth, you two wouldn't be in this situation."

Holly's dark brows knitted together in confusion. "What do you mean, 'would've been the key'?"

Paul set his cup down and looked at them for a second in surprise. "She's dead," he blurted out.

Holly's face blanched as she cupped her hands over her nose and mouth. "I checked her pulse, she was alive...I didn't kill her."

Jamie jumped up from her seat and reached out to Holly. Tears poured from her eyes as Holly slapped her hands away and ran out the door. "I have to go to her, Paul, please stay with Eden," she said as she went after Holly.

She found her friend sitting on the small pier extending slightly into the lake. Holly had her arms wrapped around herself, rocking back and forth. Jamie could hear her mournful cries long before she got near her. She approached slowly and gently wrapped Holly into her arms.

"I didn't kill her," Holly sobbed, shaking uncontrollably. "She was alive when we left that room. She was bleeding so much when I looked at her, but the head bleeds so profusely, I thought to myself, when I felt for a pulse. I couldn't have hit her that hard, Jamie!" Holly wailed into Jamie's chest.

"Listen to me, Holly," Jamie said as she rubbed her back. "Carmen aimed a gun at us. Had you not taken action, she may have killed one of us, if not both. It was self-defense."

Holly pulled away from Jamie and looked into her eyes. "I know she was threatening us, but I never meant to kill her," Holly said as her sobs took control of her again.

Paul watched helplessly as Holly rushed past him and climbed straight into the loft. "I'm so sorry. I thought you knew already," he said, as he sat back down at the kitchen table where Jamie joined him.

Paul reached across the table and took Jamie's smaller hands into his.

"What happened the morning you were confronted by your supervisor?" Paul asked gently.

Jamie fought back a sob as the horror of the situation settled in on her. She relayed the story as the memory of that morning washed over her, making her tremble.

"According to the news, your supervisor was found beaten to death in her office."

Jamie's eyes grew wide as her mouth fell agape. "Holly only hit her once. That hardly constitutes a beating."

"She was 'brutally' beaten to death, there were many broken bones. Whoever she called may have come in and finished the job." Paul blew out an exasperated breath. "Who knows what kind of connections they have? I think it's best that we don't involve the police just yet. You've got to stay here for a while until we can make sense of this. I don't like the idea of leaving you here alone, but someone may put two and two together and follow me here."

Paul sat quietly for a moment. "I'll still bring supplies when I can, but I'll have to be very careful and come at night from now on. You have the gun in a safe place, right?"

"I have it tucked away," Jamie said as she dried her face. "I have no doubt that I'll be able to use it if the need arises. If you would've told me that I would be in this situation two weeks ago, I would've said you were crazy. We could've handled this so much better had I only been patient and waited on Donald."

"Most people would've turned a blind eye to what was happening to that woman." He nodded in the direction of where Eden lay. "You and Holly saved her life. Had they been allowed to continue drugging her the way they were, she would've suffered some very serious neurological effects. You both risked everything to save the life of a patient. That, in my opinion, is very honorable and commands respect."

Jamie looked over at Eden who slept, oblivious to the conversation, and wondered for a moment if the woman would ever be coherent enough to understand the price they had paid.

"Donald and I are committed to doing everything in our power to help you through this. You will make it through, Jamie. Just be patient and don't do anything rash until we can figure out a way to have the people involved implicated."

Paul waited until dusk to begin his journey home. He hugged both women, silently praying that they would be safe until his return.

"Warn Donald about these people and tell him to be very careful," Jamie sobbed into his shoulder.

"Don't worry about me and Donald. You two need to help Eden recover quickly. She's the only key we have now," he admonished as he climbed into the cab of the pickup.

Holly dropped her cards onto the kitchen table. "I hate card games; why did I let you talk me into playing?"

"It was your idea, jackass," Jamie replied with a wicked grin.

"Let's keep the thing about Carmen to ourselves," Holly blurted out suddenly. "She may not understand right now."

Jamie blew out a breath. "You're probably right. She's still a little out of it."

"She deserved what she got." Holly's expression grew dark as her eyes narrowed.

Jamie looked up at her in surprise. "You don't mean that, Holly."

"She was just as guilty as the people who killed her. Carmen would be home safe and sound right now had she not gotten herself involved," Holly snapped.

Jamie opened her mouth to speak as Holly rose from the table.

"Don't say anything, Jamie, you know I'm right." Holly disappeared into the bathroom.

Jamie sat dumbstruck as she heard the water in the shower being turned on. She decided to allow Holly her privacy, knowing she was still grappling with her guilt over Carmen's death.

A flash of lightning split the night sky with a loud roar of thunder chasing right behind it. Jamie's eyes snapped open, and she realized that she had fallen asleep in the chair. She glanced over at the couch and could see Eden's face illuminated by the orange glow of the fireplace. She rose quietly and ran her hand over the face of the sleeping woman. Eden was covered in sweat and moaned at Jamie's touch to her fevered brow.

Jamie dampened a cloth in the bathroom and returned to Eden's side. She wiped her face and neck and listened to Eden whimper in her sleep. The next round of medications was not for four hours, and Jamie wondered how bad it would get before then.

Jamie listened as she heard the wind blow hard through the pines above the silent cabin. Lightning flashed like a strobe light through the windows, and she heard the rain splatter against the glass as the storm moved fully upon them. She worried for Paul, hoping that he had made it safely to his destination. She knew that Paul did not live in Wilmington but neglected to ask exactly where he did reside.

"Who is Paul?" Eden asked, making Jamie jump in surprise.

"He's Donald's brother. You probably don't remember, but Donald was the doctor who performed your appendectomy a few years ago," she said as she wiped Eden's brow and watched as her eyes closed again. Eden was obviously in a sleep stupor.

"Is Laura here?" Eden asked, startling Jamie for a second time.

"Who's Laura?" Jamie asked as she switched positions and pulled Eden's head into her lap.

The dark-haired woman lay silent for a moment. "I hurt her feelings," Eden mumbled groggily.

Jamie sat for a moment, wondering if Eden was talking in her sleep or simply talking out of her head. Either way, it made no sense.

"I'm not in love with her, she needed to know the truth."

Jamie's eyes flew open as she stared down at Eden, who looked back up with unfocused eyes. "Sometimes the truth is best, even if it hurts," she said as she stroked Eden's hair.

"She was so angry," Eden whispered as her eyes fluttered shut.

Jamie leaned her head back against the couch and was about to drift off to sleep when she felt Eden latch onto her and snuggle in closer. "You're safe now," she whispered, and watched the tension in Eden's face ebb.

Holly climbed down the ladder quietly so as not to disturb the two sleeping women. She started a pot of coffee to brew and walked over to the sofa where Jamie still slept with Eden's head in her lap. She studied them both for a moment until Jamie's eyes slowly opened.

Holly whispered, "Grab a cup of coffee and meet me on the porch."

Jamie gently got up from her spot without waking Eden. She stretched sore muscles, silently swearing to herself that she would not sleep in that position again. After a quick trip to the bathroom and the coffeepot, she joined Holly on the porch.

"Don't you think you're getting in a little deep with her?" She asked suddenly as Jamie took a seat.

"Frankly, I don't see how we could be in any deeper," Jamie snapped.

"I think you're a little more attached than I am," Holly shot back as calmly as she could. "I think your feelings for her are becoming more than those of just a concerned caregiver."

"That's the most absurd thing I've ever heard you say. I'm doing my best to keep her as calm and as comfortable as I can. How you can get that confused with anything else is beyond me!"

"Not from where I'm standing," Holly stated resolutely. "I don't think you realize it, and that's what really concerns me."

"Well, keep your concerns to yourself. I'm a big girl and I don't need you trying to play mother to me," Jamie said as Holly dumped her coffee and went back inside.

Jamie sat fuming at the accusation for a while, then decided on a walk before she had to face Holly again. She realized that tensions were running high and she and Holly would need their space for a little while. As she began to calm, she wondered about Holly's accusations.

She couldn't deny the surprise the night before when Eden basically confessed that she was involved with another woman—a woman Eden admitted she was not in love with. To say the least, she was intrigued.

She found Eden physically attractive, there was no denying that either. The woman was cocky and often difficult, but her looks stirred something in Jamie that she fought hard to suppress. She thought about how she treated Eden and wondered if she would be the same way with any other patient in the same situation. She decided to cool it where Eden was concerned to keep her and Holly from getting the wrong idea.

"I'll beat your ass if you do that again!" Jamie heard Holly scream from the top of her lungs as she entered the cabin. Walking into the living room, she noticed food splattered all over the floor. Eden stood in the middle of the room heaving in anger.

"Don't you ever lay a hand on me again!" Eden screamed back.

Holly looked at Jamie as she stood dumbfounded, taking in the scene before her. "What's going on here?"

"I was trying to get her to eat something and she went nuts on me," Holly hissed as she brushed the breakfast from her clothes.

Eden pressed her palms to her forehead. "I overreacted and I'm sorry. I woke up and you were standing over me, and for a moment, I forgot where I was. You just scared me."

Holly paced for a moment, trying to regain her composure. "I could've handled that better. I'm sorry. The next time, I'll wake you up before I approach you with a loaded breakfast tray."

Jamie chuckled. "I think we're all a little on edge, and for what it's worth, Holly, I'm sorry about this morning."

Eden watched as the two women exchanged glances and the tension seemed to leave the room. She knelt down and began picking up the food and dishes. Normally, Jamie would have been quick to help, but she watched in silence as Eden slowly cleaned the mess. Holly took the dishes from Eden and helped her to the sofa.

Jamie studied Eden as she sank back onto the couch, her exhaustion apparent. Her color had improved, but her hands still shook as she ran shaking fingers through her hair.

"I'm really sorry," Eden said, knowing that Jamie was watching her every move. "I'm disoriented when I wake up..." She paused a moment to regain her composure. Turning misty eyes upon Jamie, she sighed. "I'm not crazy, just a little on edge."

"I still think you should try and eat something," Holly said as she returned to Eden's side. "You're finished with the meds now, and I'm a little concerned about how your body is going to react being on its own."

"If I promise to be a good girl, can I take a shower?" Eden asked sarcastically, feeling as though they were thinking she was truly a nutcase.

"Of course, but one of us will have to help you. You're a little weak to be trying it alone," Holly responded, cocking her eyebrow at Jamie as she made her way to the kitchen.

Chapter Seven

Susan sat at her desk, staring at the name on the paper in front of her. It had been given to her a long time ago, and she wondered if the person was still alive, given his profession. Laura had not managed to take nearly enough money to support them for the rest of their lives. What she had transferred wouldn't last one of them, let alone both of them, for a year. She needed enough money to disappear permanently.

Unlike her father, whose footsteps she had been forced to follow, she was not a successful psychiatrist. In truth, she hated what she did for a living. Her intelligence alone had gotten her through medical school; she had no drive or determination. She had taken over the family practice and had nearly driven it into the ground to the disgust of her parents.

She had reduced her patient load out of sheer laziness. In the last year, the receptionist who had worked for her father for twenty years resigned when her paychecks became sporadic. Susan hated the life that had been forced upon her and did her best to make sure everyone around her suffered as a result.

Her drug use had gotten out of control. She used to be able to occasionally escape her dismal life when she got high, now it only added to her misery.

She saw straight through Laura's seduction but used it to her advantage. She had great sex with a woman who people practically stopped and stared at when she entered a room. The ultimate prize was the money, and all she had to do was make a wealthy, perfectly sane woman appear crazy.

It was so easy at first. Laura had done the dirty work. She had been the one to slip the drugs into Eden's drink. They tucked her into one of the many clinics owned by Laura's family without all the red tape and paperwork. No one asked questions, except Carmen, who took the bribe and became part of the scheme with no hesitation.

Now things were complicated. She was in too deep to turn back now, and the blonde slut who had cooked up the scheme was going to ride it out with her. With Eden supposedly abducted, the feds would no doubt be monitoring her accounts. Their little transfer plan had come to a complete stop. The solution to the problem was simple; Eden and her new friends would have to be permanently silenced.

"I think it's your turn to take bathing detail, Holly," Jamie protested. "Besides, this morning, you accused me of being too close to her, and now you're going to send me into a room with her naked."

"That's not the kind of 'close' I'm implying. I think you're beginning to care a little too much for her. I'm not worried about you groping her in the shower," Holly teased.

"It's your turn," Jamie said seriously. Her stomach muscles tightened, thinking about being in that tiny bathroom with a very naked woman who she found very attractive.

"Let's flip for it," Holly said as she groped her empty pockets for a coin.

"I don't have any change, bitch, and if anything is going to be flipped, it's gonna be you if you don't get into that bathroom right now," Jamie challenged.

"Okay, okay, we'll do it together," Holly conceded.

Eden brushed her teeth with an audience. The two nurses flanked her as she stood at the sink. "I'm not gonna make a break for it, you know," Eden said after rinsing her mouth.

"You're still weak. I've been watching your knees bang together the whole time you've been standing here," Holly said as she handed Eden a hand towel.

"Granted, I'm still weak and you're both nurses, but wouldn't you be uncomfortable trying to bathe under such scrutiny?"

"You don't have anything we don't have," Holly said with a chuckle.

"Yes, but mine doesn't look just like yours," Eden shot back. "They're all different, you know."

"Hells bells, you two! Can we just get on with this?" Jamie interjected testily.

"At least turn your backs until I can get into the shower," Eden pleaded.

After Eden closed the curtain, Jamie glared at Holly. "If you would've just come in here by yourself, she wouldn't be so uncomfortable," she hissed under her breath.

"How are you doing in there, Eden?" Holly called out, while smirking at Jamie.

Eden failed to respond for a moment, and Holly and Jamie exchanged concerned glances.

"I'm a little queasy. I think it's the hot water," Eden said.

Jamie pulled back the curtain a little and looked in on Eden, careful to keep her eyes on her patient's face. "This would've been so much easier if this place had a bathtub," Eden groaned.

"You're not going to be able to do this by yourself," Holly said over Jamie's shoulder. "Jamie will help you, and I'll step out and give you a little privacy."

Jamie's face flushed red with anger as Holly winked. "I'll find you some clothes to wear," she called out before closing the door.

Jamie struggled to get a grip on her anger at Holly while she tried to figure out the best way to assist Eden. Her heart rate jumped up a few notches as she considered the intimacy of the situation. "I needed to wash these clothes anyway," Jamie joked, as she stepped into the shower stall fully clothed.

She couldn't help notice the way Eden's eyes widened, then avoided hers as she stepped in. "Have you washed your hair yet?" she asked nervously. Eden didn't utter a word but simply shook her head no. Jamie poured shampoo in the palm of her hand and began to massage it into Eden's hair.

Eden stood perfectly still with her back turned to Jamie, as she washed and rinsed her hair. She didn't move an inch as Jamie repeated the process with the conditioner. Jamie's hands shook as she soaped up the washcloth. "Turn around so I can get your face," she said, hoping her voice didn't give away the nervousness she felt inside. "The rest I can do with your back to me."

After Eden's face had been rinsed, she turned and faced the wall, using her arms to brace herself. Jamie lifted her hair in one hand and cleaned her neck and shoulders with the other. After rinsing her shoulders, Jamie released her hair and soaped the washcloth again, using the time to gather courage for what she was about to do next.

She washed each of Eden's arms, painfully mindful that she had to press her body against Eden's to complete the task. She could feel Eden trembling against her, and she mentally reminded herself that she was shaking from having to stand so long. Jamie swallowed hard as she ran the cloth down Eden's chest and breasts, then around to her back. Eden was silent through the whole process.

She soaped her entire back and reached around to do the same to her abdomen, wondering if Eden would object to her moving farther down. When no protest was heard, she took a deep breath and ran the cloth between her legs and across her backside. Kneeling onto the shower floor, she was eye level with the most perfect rear end she had ever seen. She ran the cloth down the back of Eden's right thigh all the way to her ankle and slowly made her way up the front of the long leg. She swallowed hard when she accidentally brushed against the apex of Eden's thighs with the back of her hand.

Jamie repeated the process on the other leg as quickly as she could. She hoped that Eden could not feel her trembling as she helped her rinse off. Her voice was raspy when she did find the courage to speak. "I think we're done here."

"Thank you," Eden replied, averting her eyes. Jamie took her hand and helped her out of the shower. "There's a towel on the counter just to your right," she nearly whispered. She watched as Eden dried and wrapped her body in the towel, wondering how she would rid herself of the wet clothes and maintain her own dignity.

"Are you going to stand there and soak the floor or are you going to take off those wet clothes?" Eden asked as she dropped the lid on the toilet and sat while brushing through her hair.

"I was going to wait until you were finished. I'm sure Holly has something for you to wear," Jamie replied nervously.

"Well, I'm a little tired from my shower. I think I'll sit here for a minute," Eden said with a sardonic grin. "It's a little different when the shoe is on the other foot, isn't it?"

Jamie huffed and tugged at her wet shirt. "We weren't intentionally trying to make you uncomfortable. Hell, Eden, you didn't even have the strength to bathe yourself. What kind of people would we be if we just let you come in here alone?"

"I understand that, and I'm grateful, but now you have a better understanding of how I feel." Eden made no attempt to look away from Jamie as she undressed.

Jamie hesitated a second before she tugged the wet jeans down her legs. The saturated material tugged her underwear right along with them. Unable to muster the nerve to look back at Eden, Jamie quickly grabbed a towel and covered herself before tossing her wet clothes into the shower stall.

"Wow, Eden, you look hot!" Holly teased. "You could be the cover girl for one of those sportsmen's magazines."

Eden looked down at Donald's old blue and green flannel shirt that hung nearly to her knees. It was complemented by a pair of red sweatpants that were at least two inches too short. "It's what all the hot babes are wearing this fall, you're just jealous," Eden shot back.

"I'm going to try and wash our clothes in the bathroom sink," Jamie said as she climbed down from the loft wearing clothes that were two sizes too big. "We're not going to have anything to change into if I don't."

"I know what you mean. I've been going commando for days now," Holly said without shame.

"You can wash your own damn underwear, Holly Patton," Jamie growled, still irritated about being abandoned in the bathroom.

Holly grinned at Eden. "She loves me."

"I can tell," Eden replied with a smirk.

Boredom, stress, and living in close quarters were seriously beginning to get to Jamie. She tried her best to walk a mile or two each day, hoping to speed along the endless days. Her heart sank each time Paul didn't show with news. She felt as though she was living on another planet, with no hope of rescue.

To make matters worse, Eden and Holly clashed on everything. Not a day passed when the two were not at each other's throats and Jamie was forced to play referee. They had all succumbed to cabin fever and were feeling the strain.

Jamie walked along the trail toward the cabin, enjoying the solitude when she heard raised voices coming from the porch. She sighed heavily and made her way quickly up the hill.

"You don't have to watch me eat it!" Eden screamed. "Stick your nose back into your book and mind your own business!"

Jamie climbed the steps to the porch and looked at the two women who were behaving like children. "What's the problem now?" she asked as she took a seat on the top step.

Holly sat in the porch swing with a book in her lap. "She's dipping pickles in her Pepsi!" Holly responded in disgust.

"Like I said, you don't have to eat it or watch me while I do it," Eden seethed.

Jamie chuckled. "Well, Eden, it is gross."

"To each her own," Eden said as she stuffed the dill spear into the glass and slurped the soda from it loudly.

"Look, we have to try and get along," Jamie said, eyeing them both. "We're in a stressful situation as it is, let's not make it any harder."

Holly expelled a frustrated breath and went back to reading.

"What does that taste like?" Jamie asked as Eden bit into the pickle.

"It's sweet and sour. Wanna give it a try?" Eden asked as she held up her glass.

"I think I'll pass. How did you ever come up with the idea to do that?" Jamie grimiced as she watched Eden dip the pickle back into her glass.

"I don't know," Eden answered as she dipped the pickle again and looked at Holly with an impish grin. "I just figured it would taste good, so I tried it."

Holly growled and stuffed her nose back into her book.

"What can we do today to entertain ourselves?" Jamie thought outloud, trying to think of something to take up the rest of the day.

Holly lowered her book and leveled her gaze on Jamie. "I plan to lie here and read. Why don't you take pickle puss for another walk?"

"When I get my strength back, you're in for one hell of an ass whipping," Eden said angrily as Jamie stood and tugged at her arm.

Jamie waited until they were beyond Holly's range of hearing to speak to Eden, who walked slowly beside her. "Why do you always argue with Holly? Don't you like her?"

"That woman always seems to find a way to push my buttons," Eden replied in exasperation. "I don't normally behave like this. I guess I'm just a little grumpy."

The two walked slowly in silence until they reached the small pier jutting into the water. Eden found a spot on the wooden structure and dangled her feet over the side. Jamie sat next to her and inhaled the light breeze blowing in off the water.

"Holly just likes to tease. When she knows something gets under your skin, she goes in for the kill."

"Well, I haven't been totally innocent myself. I think irritating her has been entertaining," Eden said with a chuckle.

Jamie laughed. "When we worked together, I would drop things into her soda. She would spit it all over the place when a raisin or a peanut hit her teeth."

"I'd probably enjoy working with someone like you. I have a vague recollection of what my daily life was like, and there wasn't much laughter."

"Do you find that you're remembering more now?" Jamie asked hopefully.

Eden shook her head and stared back at the water. "Mostly just tidbits here and there. A little more comes back each day. I feel like the fog is finally starting to clear from my head."

"It might help if you write down things you remember, then maybe the pieces will come together."

Eden exhaled loudly and ran her fingers through her hair. "I guess I should. Sometimes I wonder if it's even worth remembering. The more that comes to mind makes me think I'm better off here."

"You probably feel pretty safe out here," Jamie offered as she reached down and ran her fingertips over the surface of the water.

"Part of me wants some sort of normalcy back, and the other part of me feels kind of content here. Even though my world is upside down, I feel kind of at home here."

"Well, at any other time, I'd find this place a slice of heaven. It's so serene and beautiful," Jamie said as she flicked her wet fingertips at Eden playfully.

Eden turned and looked into her eyes. "That may be it, or maybe it's just you."

Jamie's face flushed, and she turned away from Eden's gaze. "I'm glad I make you feel safe."

The moment was broken by a loud crack of gunfire. Eden and Jamie sat stunned as their disbelieving ears tried to make sense of what they heard.

"Get up here now!" Holly yelled from the porch.

Jamie jumped to her feet and helped Eden up; they made their way quickly to the cabin as Holly ran down to help them. Another shot broke the silence of the tranquil lake, and all three dropped to the ground.

"We've got to keep moving," Holly commanded as she nearly dragged Eden across the ground. Once inside the cabin, they each took a window and tried to see where the shots were coming from. Jamie cautiously looked through the window that overlooked the lake and noticed two men standing at the tree line in the distance. "I see them!"

Holly and Eden joined her cautiously. "I think they're hunters," Jamie said with a sigh of relief.

Holly wasn't as easily convinced. "How do we know that for sure?"

"Because if they were coming here to kill us, they wouldn't have shot at us from so far away and alerted us to their presence. Besides, look at them, they're just standing there. Don't you think they would be a little stealthier?" Jamie argued.

"I think you should get the gun," Holly said as she watched the strangers.

"You have a gun?" Eden interrupted.

Holly and Jamie exchanged glances.

Eden's eyes narrowed. "Ah, so you're afraid to admit to the nutcase that you have a gun."

"You're not a nutcase, and to be honest, I forgot all about the thing," Jamie said as she opened the linen closet and pulled out the revolver.

"By any chance, were you carrying that thing the day you two liberated me from the nut house?" Eden asked as she looked nervously at the weapon.

"No, but if we had, things might've turned out differently," Holly said from the window.

Jamie cocked her head to the side. "How so?"

Holly grinned. "I would've shot Eden in the ass the first time she took a swing at me."

Eden turned to Jamie. "I'll cook for the rest of the time we're stuck here if you'll just shoot one of her toes off."

Jamie chuckled at them both. "I'll just put this in a safe place, so the two of you won't start shooting each other's appendages off."

Dinner that evening was more relaxed, and Eden did her best to make polite conversation. "Are either of you married?" she asked. She noticed how Jamie avoided the topic.

"I was almost married," Holly said as she pushed her empty plate away. "I woke up one morning and realized he was an asshole. Took me five years to figure that out, so I sent him packing, and I've been happy ever since."

Eden looked at Jamie, who toyed with the remainder of food on her plate. When she glanced up, she noticed that Eden was looking at her expectantly.

"I've never been interested in marriage. I guess I've never met the right one. The people I've dated weren't interested in anything serious either. I suppose that's what drew me to them in the first place. And I absolutely hate wedding ceremonies. Had my mom not stepped in, I wouldn't have gone to my sister's wedding."

Holly threw her head back and bellowed with laughter. "Jamie had an admirer back at the facility."

Jamie's face flushed red. "Shut up, Holly."

"He used to follow her around all during her shift watching everything she did."

Jamie groaned. "He was an old man who didn't even know where he was."

Holly continued with a wicked gleam in her eye. "One day, he approached Jamie in the hall. She was always cheerful, and she greeted him with a big smile. He walked right up to her and grabbed both her boobs."

Jamie rolled her eyes in embarrassment. "I reacted and shoved him into the wall before I could stop myself. No one saw him grab me but Holly. Everyone thought I was just roughing up the old guy."

Eden laughed right along with Holly, who explained that the old man wore a grin on his face from that day forward.

"See what a wonderful nurse you are? You made that guy's stay a happy one," Eden teased.

"What about you, Eden, anyone special in your life?" Holly asked as she dabbed away the tears of laughter.

The smile faded from Eden's face. "No, not anymore," she answered softly.

Holly and Jamie noticed the swift mood change. "I'm sorry, did I bring up something sensitive?" Holly offered.

Eden smiled weakly. "It might be if I could remember all of it."

Holly reached across the table and patted Eden on the hand. "Don't worry, it'll all come back to you soon enough."

Eden sighed. "One of the things I do remember is the feeling of elation and wonder when I met my first girlfriend in college. It's been so long since I felt that way about anyone, and sometimes I'm afraid I'll never feel it again. Do you think that breathtaking feeling passes when we mature and go through different relationships, or will it happen again when we meet that special someone?"

"I think the wonder of the first love is unique," Holly responded sincerely. "But I don't think we grow out of the feelings we get when we meet that someone who turns us inside out."

Jamie sat silently listening and wasn't prepared to say anything until Holly pulled her into the conversation. "What about you, Jamie?"

"The wonder of it all has faded over the years for me. Now when I meet a prospective partner, I tend to look at things a little more logically. If I met my first love for the first time right now, I'd run the other way." Jamie smiled. "Way too many issues with that one, but when I was younger, I just didn't see it."

"But you've met people who have really rung your bells since then, haven't you?" Holly asked as she got up to clear the table.

Jamie's face colored, and she could feel Eden's eyes on her, but she dared not return the gaze. "Yes, I have met someone who has turned me to jelly, but I'm not sure they were the best for me, so I didn't pursue anything further."

"Well, I guess that person didn't realize the opportunity they missed," Eden said softly before getting up from the table.

Jamie watched Eden walk slowly across the room, and butterflies filled her stomach.

The following morning, Eden joined Holly on the porch as Jamie puttered around the kitchen. The sound of the door nearly being jerked from the hinges startled them both as Jamie walked brusquely onto the porch.

"Are you comfortable, Eden?" Jamie asked suddenly.

"Yes, very," Eden replied, trying to figure out why Jamie's face was so flushed.

"Great, because I need Holly's help with the stove, I can't get it to light. Will you be okay out here for a few minutes?"

"I'm a big girl," Eden said before sipping her coffee.

Holly got up and joined Jamie in the kitchen. Jamie picked up the cell phone that Paul had left for emergencies. "This has been used; do you know anything about it?" she asked accusingly.

Holly looked sheepishly at the floor. "I made a quick call to a friend and asked her to let my family know I'm all right."

Jamie slammed her hand down on the counter. "How could you be so irresponsible? This was for emergencies only! And furthermore, your phone call wasn't quick at all; fifteen minutes are registered on this phone."

Holly countered angrily. "It was an emergency for me to let my parents know that I'm okay. They're old folks, Jamie, and I didn't want one of them dying of a heart attack worrying about me!"

"You should've discussed this with me first! We're in this situation together, and I should've been consulted at the very least."

"I don't have to ask your permission to do anything."

"Consulting and asking permission are two different things," Jamie spat.

"Look, we've been under a lot of pressure and things have been tense around here for a few days," Holly said, reining in her temper. "I'm going to take a walk and cool down before things escalate."

The door slammed behind her.

Jamie leaned against the counter, letting tears of frustration and anger stream down her face. There were many times she considered calling her family to let them know she was still alive. She worried constantly about what they were thinking and the interrogations that they had surely faced.

It hurt her deeply thinking that they may have been chastised by people who believed she was capable of molesting a patient, then kidnapping her. She turned the phone in her hand and stared at it, wondering what it would hurt to take the same liberties that Holly had.

The back door creaked open and Eden crept slowly inside. "I think you two may need a break from each other for a while," she said as she sank into one of the kitchen chairs.

"Well, unless there's a tent stashed away around here, there isn't much hope of that," Jamie replied bitterly as she tucked the phone into a drawer before Eden could catch sight of it.

"Do you want to vent on me for a little while?" Eden asked with a shy smile.

"I think cabin fever has taken its toll on us," Jamie said as she wiped her eyes. "Holly and I have bickered the last couple of days, and I guess a blowout was unavoidable."

Eden bowed her head. "I guess it's not a good time for this, but I wanted to say thank you for what you've done for me. You've both risked everything for a total stranger, and had I been in your shoes, I'm not sure I would've had the fortitude to do the same."

"To be perfectly honest, Eden, we wanted to help, but neither of us planned for it to turn out the way it did. Whoever is responsible for what happened to you is very vicious, and I assume well-connected. We don't have a leg to stand on until our friends come up with some answers."

"Forgive me for asking the obvious, but why didn't you just go straight to the police?"

Jamie sighed and rubbed her face. "In hindsight, we should have when we first left the center, but we were in a panic and not thinking clearly. That gave them all the time they needed to point the guilty finger at us. They've accused us of some vile things, not the least of which is kidnapping."

Eden quirked an eyebrow. "What kind of vile things?"

Jamie felt the pit of her stomach tighten, instantly regretting saying as much as she did. "They've accused us of...handling you inappropriately and kidnapping you to cover it."

"What do you mean by 'handling'?"

Jamie fought the urge to look away from Eden's inquisitive stare and hoped that Eden would see the truth in her eyes. "They've accused us of having sexual relations with you and drugging you to keep you quiet."

Eden's silence made Jamie uncomfortable, but she refused to look away. "We were never allowed anywhere near you, Eden. Carmen, the nursing supervisor, was solely responsible for your care. We weren't even allowed to see your chart. That's why we became concerned about what was happening to you. Neither Holly nor I ever laid a hand on you."

"Well, that's a good thing, I guess. I think I would've preferred to have been in my right mind if one of you wanted to paw at me a little bit," Eden said with a playful grin.

The tension of the moment ebbed, and Jamie returned the smile. "I prefer the people I 'paw' to be willing participants, so you were always safe from me."

"Am I safe from you now?" Eden asked with a raised brow.

Jamie's face colored a little. "That would depend on your willingness to participate."

Eden pulled the door open to the porch and looked back over her shoulder. "You have my permission to 'paw' at will," she said with a wink, then closed the door behind her.

Jamie stood rooted to the spot with an ear-to-ear grin plastered on her face.

"Dr. Lappin, please have a seat," Charles McManus said as she nervously entered his office. "I've called you here today to discuss Ellen Edmonds.

"As you know, the authorities are very interested in this patient." He stared across his desk at the doctor, the irritation evident in his words and demeanor. "She's a bit of an enigma. There's no file, no family has been located, and to top it all off, the woman the staff described doesn't exist. And you have yet to fill in the gaps on this patient."

"I'm aware of that, sir. The police have questioned me extensively. I'm afraid all the answers lie with Carmen. As far as I can tell, she was a friend of Carmen's, and that's how she got here in the first place."

"I keep getting that same response from you," Charles replied sharply. As the attending physician, I would expect you to have a lot more information than you're offering. The focus of the police is no longer on Carmen now but has switched to you. I'd appreciate not having to contend with any more ugly surprises. Is there anything else you would like to tell me?"

"No, sir, I've told you all I know."

Charles knew that Susan was hiding something and tried another approach. "Susan, you have to realize how bad this looks for us. There are no computer records on this woman, and her patient file mysteriously disappeared with her. We're looking at a lawsuit when her family catches wind of this. And don't be mistaken, you won't emerge from this unscathed. As I said before, you were the only physician treating Ellen Edmonds. I strongly suggest you retain an attorney and seek legal counsel."

"I'm already looking into that," Susan replied as she stood to leave. "Is there anything else you'd like to discuss?"

Charles sighed and tugged his glasses from his face. "No, Susan, I guess not."

"Thank you for seeing me, Detective Salamoni," Al Pittman greeted the detective as he offered her a seat.

"My captain said it was imperative that I meet with you. I'm very sorry that our department has failed to accommodate you thus far," the attractive detective said as she took a seat.

Al studied the woman sitting before him intently. Unlike the detective he had spoken with before, she was a professional, evident by the way she presented herself. Tiny lines around her eyes belied her youthful appearance, and he surmised she was around Eden's age. She neither fidgeted nor looked away from his scrutiny. Her intelligent brown eyes looked back at him and conveyed that she was aware he was sizing her up.

Al assumed that the tailored blazer concealed a well-toned body, unlike her pudgy predecessor. She cocked an eyebrow, waiting patiently for him to continue.

"Your captain and I go way back. I've known him before he ever joined the force here. He assured me that you would handle the situation to my satisfaction," Al said firmly.

The detective opened the file she held and began to read. "Let's go over what we have so far. Miss Carlton has been missing for nearly three and a half months. Her assistant claimed to have received emails stating she was away on vacation, but you've had no contact with her whatsoever." She read the file quietly for a moment. "Help me understand in what capacity you work for Miss Carlton."

"I've worked for her grandfather for many years, and when Eden took over the company, I became her employee. I privately audit her accounts. No one in her office is aware of my presence. I make sure that there's no embezzlement, and I advise her on her holdings." Al accepted a cup of tea from his housekeeper and offered the detective one, as well.

"There are a couple of reasons why I believe Eden is in trouble. The first being that Eden is like a daughter to me, and we are in constant contact. She would never leave without making me aware of what she was doing. The second is that I've found some inconsistencies in her accounts. Without going into great detail, I've found quite a few companies that I don't recognize receiving large amounts of funds. The specifics are in the report you're holding."

Detective Salamoni cleared her throat. "As you've requested, we've done some research on Miss Carlton. There's no record of her leaving the country. And since you've made it clear that you believe her assistant is involved, we've been doing some research on her, as well. Were you aware that Miss Carlton was intimately involved with Laura McManus?"

Al perked up. "Where did you come up with this?"

"We questioned some of the people you said were Miss Carlton's friends. All of them volunteered that she and Miss McManus were seeing each other romantically."

Al sat quietly stunned at the revelation. "Have you questioned Miss McManus?"

"We have and she stated that Miss Carlton felt the relationship was getting too intense too soon, and she needed time away to sort things out." The detective watched as Al rubbed his chin and pondered what he was hearing.

"We've done a little background check on Miss McManus. She's the daughter of Charles McManus, who owns several mental health clinics throughout the Carolinas. Two weeks ago, one of his patients was kidnapped by a couple of nurses on his staff. The mysterious thing is that there was no patient file on this woman. Furthermore, we've run a check on the patient's name and have come up with one hundred thirty-seven people with that name, and they're all accounted for."

Al's eyes grew wide. "And you think there might be a connection with Eden and this patient?"

"Well, I find it interesting that Miss Carlton supposedly went on vacation and has been away around the same time this patient was admitted to the clinic, according to the staff. And that the clinic is owned by the father of her assistant. Do you have a picture of Miss Carlton that I can take with me to the clinic?"

Al stood and walked to the mantel and lovingly grasped the frame to his chest. "This is my Eden."

After the detective left, Al poured himself a brandy and sat at his desk, silently scolding himself for ignoring what he knew in his heart. Perhaps if he would have come to terms with Eden's sexuality sooner, he may have been able to shield her from the woman who was possibly responsible for her disappearance.

Tension between Holly and Jamie at the dinner table was palpable that evening. The three of them ate in near silence. Eden watched the interaction between the other women closely. She wasn't sure what they had fought about earlier, but silence between them was becoming intolerable to Eden, who sat between them.

"Pass the salt," Jamie nearly growled.

Without looking in Jamie's direction, Holly pushed the shaker away from her plate.

"Dinner is delicious...although I'm not exactly sure what it is," Eden offered with a chuckle.

Jamie glanced up at Eden. "We're running a little low on choices, so I just threw some things together in a pot."

"Let's name it 'low choice stew' then," Eden said, looking at Holly, waiting for one of her typical sarcastic responses. "Um, Holly, do you have any suggestions?"

Holly looked directly at Jamie. "We could call it shit stew because that's exactly what it tastes like."

Eden laughed until she noticed Jamie and Holly glaring at each other across the table. "Okay, Jamie, it's your turn to come up with a name," Eden said meekly before taking another bite.

Jamie turned angry eyes to Eden. "It's just damn stew, let's call it that."

"Damn stew it is then," Eden said with a nervous laugh. "I'm much better now, so I think you both can share the bed upstairs. I'm sure you're tired of sleeping in that recliner."

"I'm more than happy with the recliner," Jamie said curtly.

Holly set her spoon down. "Fair is fair, the bed is yours tonight, Jamie. I'll take the recliner."

Silence once again fell upon them as they ate.

Chapter Eight

Susan looked at her fake passport for the tenth time, silently hoping that there would be no complications. Laura sat next to her, drumming her fingers on the armrest as they waited for their flight. Too nervous to speak, they sat quietly as they waited for the boarding call.

Things were not going according to plan for Laura—she never intended for Susan to leave the country with her. But Susan stuck to her like glue and made it impossible for her to skip out alone. She wondered how she would rid herself of the doctor before it was time to withdraw the money she'd stashed away.

Too much heat surrounded them for Laura to wait any longer. With each passing day, they were running out of answers for the police and her father. She was afraid Susan would crack under the pressure, so she decided to skip the country with her in tow. There would be time to deal with her once they were safely out of the U.S.

Jamie sipped her first cup of coffee as Eden began to stir. "Good morning," she said as Eden sat up and wiped her hair from her eyes. "I've got homemade biscuits baking; they shouldn't be long. Are you feeling strong enough to make it to the bathroom alone?"

"Yeah, I feel pretty good this morning," Eden said as she stretched.

"I'm going to go find Holly. She's probably out for her morning walk. Breakfast will be ready in about ten minutes," Jamie said as she headed for the door.

Eden emerged from the bathroom to an empty cabin. She walked slowly to the kitchen and took the biscuits out of the oven before they burned. She noticed the bacon sitting on a plate next to the stove and grabbed a piece. She nibbled the salty delight while looking out the window and noticed Jamie coming up the path alone.

Whatever they had fought about the day before must have been serious, she assumed, as she noted the grimace on Jamie's face.

"No luck?" Eden asked as Jamie came through the door.

"I couldn't find her on the trail..." Jamie paused in mid-sentence before rushing back out the door. Eden watched as she ran to the side of the cabin, then came walking back slowly.

"What's wrong?" Eden asked as Jamie walked back in and slammed the door.

"She left us! She took the damn van and left us here!" Jamie screamed as she paced back and forth. She glimpsed a piece of paper sitting on top of a neatly folded blanket left on the recliner. Jamie snatched the note and read aloud.

Dear Jamie,
I couldn't take it anymore. Please stay put and I'll find a way to get word to you when the coast is clear. I'm so sorry.
Holly

Susan did her best to act casual as they stood in line to board the plane. She clutched her boarding pass and gritted her teeth against the nausea burning in her stomach. Her nerves always affected her this way. She glanced over at Laura, who looked calm and collected.

"Ladies, I'm going to have to ask you to step out of the line, please."

Susan's head snapped toward the voice. A man in a suit holding a badge flanked by two uniformed officers stood looking at her. With nowhere to run, Susan obeyed the order.

Susan glanced over at Laura as they were being read their rights and patted down. She had never wanted to kill someone so badly in her entire life until that moment. Her eyes fell upon the holstered weapon on the hip of the officer checking Laura. She had nothing to lose at this point in the game. She grimaced when her hands were pulled down and cuffed before she was able to act on her impulse.

Jamie sat on the porch with her head in her hands as Eden joined her. They both sat quietly for a while before either spoke.

"Why don't we just hike up to the main road and get someone to call the police? I'm lucid now and can testify that I wasn't kidnapped," Eden said softly.

"You're not strong enough to make that hike, Eden. Besides there are some things you don't know," Jamie said with a sigh.

"Fill me in."

Jamie debated for a moment. She had already been thinking about how she would explain their situation. "Remember when I told you that Holly dealt with Carmen when we took you from the center that day?"

Eden nodded and waited patiently for the rest.

"When we left, she was alive, but Paul informed us that she had been beaten to death. I don't believe for a second that Holly hit her hard enough to kill her. It's not just the police we've been hiding from out here."

Donald opened his door to a clean-cut man waving a badge. "May I help you?" he asked politely.

"Dr. Donald Briggs?" the man inquired.

"I am," he responded as he opened the door and allowed the man in his home.

"If you have a moment, I'd like to ask you a few questions. I'm Detective Mason."

"I've already given a formal statement, but I'll answer whatever questions you may have," Donald said as he poured himself and the officer a cup of coffee.

"I need to know if you've heard from Miss Spencer since she left the clinic."

"No, I haven't heard a word from her. Do you have any news, detective?" Donald asked as he set the coffee down in front of Mason.

"No, sir, we don't have anything yet. We have a few leads, but I was hoping you had heard from her."

"I can assure you, Detective Mason, that Jamie is a good woman, and I'm certain that she'll be able to prove her innocence. This is totally out of character for her."

"How long have you known Miss Spencer, Dr. Briggs?"

"I've known her for a few years. She was a nurse at the hospital where we both worked. She was a very compassionate woman and an excellent nurse—someone you could call upon in a pinch."

"How would you describe your relationship with Miss Spencer?" the detective asked as he sipped his coffee.

"I consider her a very dear friend."

"Was your relationship strictly platonic?"

Donald set his cup down with a thud, and coffee splashed onto the table. "That is very inappropriate. If you have anything more you would like to ask, you'll have to bring me in for questioning," Donald said as he stood. "For now, I'll show you to the door."

Donald strode from the room without looking back. Mason hopped up and followed closely on his heels. Donald never saw him pick up the vase from the hallway table. The blow knocked him to the floor, and the last thing he saw before he left this life was the smiling picture of his wife. He smiled in relief knowing that he would be seeing her soon.

"So now we sit and wait for what?" Eden asked, reeling from the information that Jamie had given her.

"We wait for Dr. Briggs and his brother Paul to give us the all clear," Jamie responded sullenly. "Can you think of anything that would help us at all?"

Eden stood and walked to the edge of the porch and looked out over the lake. She closed her eyes, replaying the bits and pieces of her memory that had returned to her. "What was the name of the place where I was being held?"

"McManus Mental Health Center," Jamie replied.

"To be honest, I remembered you telling me that when we first got here." Eden's shoulders slumped as she sighed. "My ex-girlfriend's father owns several mental health clinics. Her name is Laura McManus. When you first told me it was a McManus clinic I was being held in, I just didn't want to believe that Laura could've done this to me, and I was too ashamed to admit it to you. She had to have had a hand in this."

"Well, I suppose that explains how you ended up there, but why?"

"I have no clue. I'm not crazy, and I didn't have a drug problem before I got there, so I have no idea why I was put in such a place." She turned suddenly and looked at Jamie. "You do believe that I'm not insane, don't you?"

"I know you're not insane, Eden," Jamie said softly.

Eden nodded, seemingly satisfied with her answer.

Jamie stood and walked over to Eden where she gently took her arm. "You feel up to taking a walk?"

Eden walked along the leaf-laden path, enjoying the way they sounded as they crunched under her feet. The sun felt good on her skin, as the autumn breeze caused the serene water on the lake to ripple.

"I wasn't in love with her, and I was honest with her about it," she said out of the blue. "I should've ended it a long time ago, but…she met certain needs."

"So you stayed with her just for sex?" Jamie asked bluntly.

"It wasn't just the sex, it was companionship. I knew I could never be in anything long term with her, but spending time with her chased away some of the loneliness." Eden paused for a moment and looked Jamie in the eye.

"When you're wealthy, it's hard to make true friends, and it's even harder to find someone who isn't interested solely in your assets. We had that in common, but Laura was very social and loved to be in the spotlight. That was something we didn't share. I hated all the fake smiles and pretentious attitudes."

"So money was the only thing you two had in common?" Jamie asked as Eden resumed the walk.

"The more time I spent with her, the lonelier I became. I felt trapped in a relationship that I knew was going nowhere. Regardless of how much I pulled away from her, she only clutched on tighter, until I had to be brutally honest. I don't think she realized how miserable I'd become."

Uncomfortable with the conversation, Eden changed the subject.

"So how long have you and Holly been together?"

Jamie stopped dead in her tracks. "Holly and I were never together. She's a friend and a co-worker, and that's as far as it goes. And what makes you think I'm gay?" Jamie asked defensively.

Eden smirked. "I could feel your hands trembling when you helped me take a shower."

"And from that you think I'm gay?"

"You're a nurse, and you must've bathed a thousand people by now, but you were nervous when you touched me. When you talk about dating, you speak in ambiguous terms. Those are signals our kind knows well."

Embarrassed and feeling exposed, Jamie's temper flared. "You are one big presumptuous ass, Eden Carlton," she hissed before turning on her heel and heading back to the cabin.

Eden watched as Jamie stormed away. She chuckled, then spied a nice sunny spot on the pier and made her way there.

Jamie plopped down on the couch, grinding her teeth in anger. Eden had hit the nail on the head. Her embarrassment was acute, which spurned her anger, coupled with the fact that Holly bailed out. The emotions within her collided, and she did the only thing that would bring her relief—she cried.

Detective Salamoni walked into the clinic with the picture of Eden Carlton still in its protective frame clutched tightly in her hand. The captain was riding her, and mistakes and oversights would not be tolerated. She chose to avoid the administrator's office and sought out the floor staff.

She was stopped by a large security guard who blocked her path until she showed her ID. "How long have you worked here?" she asked the burly man as she noted the name displayed on his nametag.

"I was hired on when a patient was taken from the facility," he replied curtly.

Detective Salamoni looked over his shoulder and noted that there were no security cameras. "Do you know if they had any sort of security staff before the abduction?"

The guard sucked his teeth and looked at her for a moment. "You'll need to talk to administration for those answers. Like I told you, I just started here."

"Then step out of my way," she responded politely, but her expression made it clear that she would not be bullied by his intimidation tactics.

The guard held his position directly in front of her and smirked. Detective Salamoni squeezed the badge she still held in her hand. She smiled back up at the guard and smacked him in the forehead hard enough to leave the impression of her badge number on his forehead.

"Damn it, Melanie! Why do you always have to hit so hard?" the security guard groaned as he rubbed his head.

"Why do you always make me hit you, Trent?" she replied in her best girly tone.

Trent grinned. "Because you always have to rub that detective badge in my face."

"You'd have one, too, if you hadn't have shot that lady's poodle. When are you getting off probation?"

"I've got another six months," Trent sighed.

Detective Salamoni patted her former partner on the shoulder. "Hang in there, kiddo, and soon you won't have to work crummy details like this one."

"Watch your step back there. An old man grabbed some nurse's tits, then pissed on the floor," Trent called over his shoulder.

Detective Salamoni walked along the hallways slowly, making mental notes of the layout of the clinic. She paused for a moment at the sealed room that had been occupied by the patient in question, when she was finally approached by a member of the staff.

"I'm Detective Salamoni, and I have a few questions if you don't mind," the detective said as she studied the young woman in front of her. "First, were you employed here when Ellen Edmonds was a patient?"

"I've worked here for three years now, and I was on duty the morning Miss Edmonds was taken."

Detective Salamoni held up the picture, refusing to allow it from her grasp. "Does this woman look familiar to you?"

"That's her! That's Ellen Edmonds," the aide exclaimed excitedly. "Have you found her yet?"

"No, ma'am, we haven't, but this is a big help. I need to have a few more members of the staff identify her, as well. Please don't tip them off before I have a chance to speak with them."

Detective Salamoni's pulse quickened with the confirmation that her suspicions had been correct. She left the clinic with a spring in her step. Five different employees positively identified Eden as Ellen Edmonds. Life for the two women in custody was going to get far more difficult, she thought with a smile, and she would be there to watch them squirm.

Jamie wiped her face as she heard Eden walking up the wooden steps. She leaned her head back on the couch and pretended to be napping, hoping that Eden would simply leave her alone.

Eden walked into the cabin and made her way to the recliner where she sat and studied Jamie for a moment. "I'm really sorry if I offended you."

"How did you know I wasn't asleep?" Jamie asked as she lifted her head.

"If I had been as angry as you were when you came in here, it would be a very long time before I would be calm enough to fall asleep," Eden answered with a slight smile.

"You make a lot of assumptions based on how you would react," Jamie said gruffly.

"Doesn't everyone?"

"No, and not everyone is the same."

"So you're still going to sit there and deny the fact that you're gay?" Eden asked with a grin.

"Okay, damn it! I'm gay! Is that what you wanted to hear?" Jamie bellowed.

Eden sat back in the chair and crossed her legs. "Yes."

Jamie shook her head in exasperation. "I think I liked you better when you slept all the time."

"I need to feel like I can talk to you openly, and for me to be comfortable in doing that, I need you to be open with me, so no secrets. Besides, the more I talk, the more I remember."

Jamie sat up straight. "So what do you want me to tell you?"

"Simple stuff, like is there someone waiting for you to come home, besides your family? What are your hobbies? What kind of music do you listen to?" Eden said as she stood and made her way to the coffeepot.

"Eden, do you smoke?" Jamie asked from her perch on the couch.

ROBIN ALEXANDER

Chapter Nine

Mason sat in his car parked on a tree-lined street of beautiful homes that spoke of wealth and prestige. He thumbed through Donald's address book as he waited to see if anyone would emerge from Paul Briggs's home. He gazed down at the electricity bill lying next to him on the seat. If Paul had nothing to offer, he would make the drive into the country and survey Donald's vacation home.

Though he was unable to contact Susan and unaware of her arrest, he was still determined to complete his job. The money was too good to pass up, even though she hadn't yet paid him a dime. The real bonus was getting his hands on the woman in the picture that sat in his lap. There were perks to this job, and spending some time alone with the brunette would make all the travel worthwhile.

"So there's a chance that Eden is alive!" Al Pittman exclaimed excitedly as he listened to the report that Detective Salamoni relayed to him as they strolled the grounds surrounding his home.

"Now we know exactly who we're looking for," the detective answered with a smile. "I'd like to use this picture to post on the wires. Maybe someone has seen her and can give us some leads."

"Of course, use it for whatever you need. I wanted to ask you something the other day, detective, but it slipped my mind. What's your first name?"

"Melanie, but everyone just calls me Salamoni," she answered with a smile.

"May I ask if you have children?"

"I have two—a boy and a girl."

Al smiled and rubbed his weary brow. "As you know, Eden is like a daughter to me. As a mother, I'm certain you can understand why I'm so concerned for her well-being, so if I'm abrupt sometimes, please excuse this old man."

The detective paused for a moment and looked Al in the eyes. "That's precisely why I came here in person to deliver the news, Mr. Pittman. If that was one of my children out there, I would kill or die to make sure she was returned safely." She smiled and patted him on the shoulder. "I have an idea of what you may be going through, and I can assure you that finding Eden is my top priority."

Al held up his arm, and Detective Salamoni grinned as she looped her arm with his, continuing their walk.

Jamie coughed as she inhaled the sweet smoke from the pipe she had been puffing on. Eden sat across from her with one clamped in her teeth, giggling.

"It's not a cigarette, but it's kind of calming anyway," Jamie said with a snort. "I'm glad Donald left one of his pipe kits here."

"I can't picture you as a cigarette smoker," Eden said with a grin.

"I quit about three years ago," Jamie said as she enjoyed the aroma of the cherry tobacco. "This smell brings back memories of working with Donald. I miss him."

"I'm afraid I don't remember that much about him, but the way you look when you talk about him tells me that he's more than just a former co-worker."

"He taught me so much," Jamie said with a sad smile. "He took me under his wing and was like a father to me. Whenever I faced a difficult situation, he was always right there behind me, gently encouraging."

Eden stared off into the distance for a moment. Jamie's description of Dr. Briggs stirred something within her. Hazy images flittered through her mind, and she was filled with sadness and longing but unable to identify why.

Jamie watched as myriad emotions displayed on Eden's face. "Are you okay?" she asked when Eden looked as though she would cry.

"I remember more each day, but sometimes…I feel more than I remember. Just a second ago, I had such a feeling of homesickness when you were talking about Donald. I guess he just reminded me of someone I can't place yet."

"You told me about your grandfather the other day, maybe it's him you miss," Jamie offered.

"No, he passed away a long time ago. This person is in my life now."

"Well, we'll just have to keep talking to jog your memory."

Eden relit her pipe and puffed it for a moment. "Okay, we have coffee and nicotine; it's time to tell me your story."

"I've already told you about my family, that just leaves my love life, and it's null and void at the moment. So, no, there's no one waiting at home for me."

"Here's to the single life," Eden said as she raised her cup in a toast. Jamie clanked her cup with hers.

"So you like being single?" Jamie asked. "Are relationships too complicated for you?"

"I'd love to be in a relationship," Eden answered wistfully, "with someone who made my heart flutter each time she walks into a room, but I've nearly given up on such romantic notions."

"Did you feel that way about Laura when you first met her?"

Eden grimaced and looked away. "When we first met, I was actually intrigued by her arrogance. I admired how she brazenly took control of every situation and made it her own."

"How did you meet her?" Jamie asked.

"An acquaintance of mine knew someone she dated. One night, we were at dinner and Laura stopped at our table to say hello. She wound up sitting with us and having a few drinks. She was charming and extremely good looking, and before the night was over, she asked me out."

Jamie felt a twinge of jealousy when Eden admitted that Laura was good looking. It was that moment she came to terms with her attraction to Eden. She was hooked. "What's the last memory you have of Laura?"

"I remember her being very hurt and angry."

"How does that make you feel?" Jamie asked, hoping it wasn't obvious that she was prying.

Eden thought for a minute. "I felt sorry for her because I didn't mean to hurt her, but the other side of me felt relieved for telling her the truth. I just couldn't make myself feel anything for her."

"Was there anyone else who may have stolen your interest?"

Eden sighed. "No, I just wanted out."

The green-eyed monster of jealousy was rearing its ugly head, but Jamie could not stifle the desire to learn more of the woman who had shared Eden's bed. "Was the companionship you spoke of strictly sexual or was there something more?" The words were out of her mouth as quickly as they swirled through her brain, causing Jamie to look away in embarrassment.

Eden grinned with a twinkle in her eye. "Ah, you want to know if I stayed with her because the sex was great."

Jamie's face flushed red. "That was extremely personal, and I'm sorry."

Eden threw back her head and laughed. "Well, we're baring our souls here, so there's no need to be embarrassed. Yes, the sex was great. Laura was a voracious lover, but even mind-blowing great sex was not enough to make me stay with her."

The image of Eden in the arms of another woman flittered through Jamie's mind. Hands roaming over the smooth body that she had gotten a good look at filled her with jealousy and arousal. "I'm getting a little tired, how about we call it a night?" Jamie said abruptly.

Eden noticed the change but said nothing. Instead she simply gathered their things and followed Jamie inside, with a knowing smirk on her face.

As they walked in, Jamie looked up at the loft and thought of the bed. "If you're feeling strong enough to make it up the ladder, you can have the bed tonight. I'll be happy to take the couch."

"That couch has some very uncomfortable spots in it. We can share the bed. I promise not to bite," Eden said with a grin.

Jamie's heart rate sped up upon considering sharing a bed with Eden. "That's all the more reason you should have the bed to yourself. You'll sleep much better up there."

"I won't sleep any better knowing you're down here on that couch or chair."

Jamie laid her head on the pillow, careful not to get too close to the middle of the bed. Eden had already turned on her side facing away from her, and her deep breathing assured Jamie she was asleep.

Jamie lay there for a long time thinking about Holly and wondering if she was safe. When the anger cooled, the feeling of loss and sadness filled the void. She said a silent prayer for her safety just before slipping off to sleep.

When the first few rays of the dawning day fell across the bed, Jamie awoke with a start. She opened one eye and realized that her hand lay in the middle of Eden's chest. She could feel the steady heartbeat underneath her fingertips, and the urge to run her fingers over soft skin startled her. Quickly, she pulled the hand that betrayed her close to her body. She lay there for a long time looking at Eden's profile before drifting back to sleep.

Eden counted to three hundred forty while waiting for Jamie to fall back to sleep. She awoke just before Jamie and was enjoying the feel of her touch, even if she wasn't aware of it. When she felt Jamie awaken, she controlled her heartbeat by counting, afraid to give away the fact that her touch excited her.

Slowly, she crept out of bed, dressed, and made her way down the ladder with an ear-to-ear grin.

"Our pantry is looking a little bare," Jamie said as she joined Eden at the breakfast table a little later. "I hope Paul pays us a visit soon. I don't know about you, but I'm getting a little tired of soup."

"Do you like fish?" Eden asked.

"Yeah, I do, and Donald has several rods and reels in the closet. You want to try catching our dinner?" Jamie said with a smile.

"What else do we have to do with our time?" Eden replied with a wicked grin.

When Detective Salamoni and the interrogation team assimilated the pieces of the puzzle that tied Laura and Susan to Eden's disappearance, both women turned on each other. Susan was the first to confess that Laura came up with the scheme and she was the unwitting accomplice.

Laura, the more manipulative of the two, wove a tale that made her look like a lovesick fool. "I was hurt, so I went along with Susan's idea. I thought it would be a great payback for her to wake up one morning in a mental health facility." Laura paused for effect and dabbed at the tears under her eyes. "I know it was malicious, but she broke my heart. I never dreamed Susan would take it to the level she did."

She could see the empathy in the eyes of the two male detectives who questioned her, and it spurned her act on.

"After Eden was tucked away in the clinic, Susan and Carmen took over. Susan threatened to tell Eden that I had done it all, and I was afraid Eden would sue my father, so I went along with the plan," Laura said, sounding like a frightened child.

One of her attorneys rubbed the back of his emotional client as she gave her statement.

"Then one morning, Susan called and told me to get to the clinic because there was an emergency. I was terrified something bad had happened to Eden. When I arrived, I found Susan in Carmen's office. She was covered in blood and Carmen was on the floor. Susan cleaned up and gave me her clothes to dispose of while she told me that two nurses had taken Eden." Laura broke into sobs.

One of the detectives handed Laura a box of tissues while the other poured her a glass of water. They waited patiently for her to continue. Laura composed herself, silently feeling that she had them in the palm of her hand.

"Susan told me that she killed Carmen so there wouldn't be any fear of her caving in and confessing that she had taken part in our plan. She told me if I didn't continue to go along, she would kill me, too. I was so scared!" Laura screamed.

"So what did you do with her clothing?" One of the detectives asked calmly.

"I put it in a plastic bag and hid it in my house for the day when I felt I could tell the truth." Laura continued to sob as the detectives made notes and recorded the rest of her statement.

Detective Salamoni watched the conversation in disgust. She despised Laura the minute she laid eyes on her. She had heard once that it takes a genius to play a fool, and she was certain that Laura was not the innocent pawn she pretended to be.

With the damning evidence stacked against her, Susan took matters into her own hands. They found her one morning in her cell with a sheet tied securely around her neck. She never told a soul about her deal with Mason. That secret went with her to the grave. Their plan was irreversible now. Mason would not stop until Eden Carlton and her rescuers were dead.

Eden watched as the shiny spinner returned to her once again without a fish. She sighed and cast it out again. "Are you getting anything over there?" she called to Jamie, who stood at a safe distance on the bank. She rubbed at the small cut on her arm, where the spinner bait had caught her on one of Eden's many casts.

"No, you're the only one who has hooked anything," she called back with a frown.

"I'm sorry!" Eden yelled back as something hit her line. "Oh, shit!" she screamed as she began to struggle with the fish. Jamie dropped her pole and ran to her side.

"Don't let it go, Eden, keep reeling," she said excitedly as she readied the net. "Get it close to the pier and I'll grab it."

The fish flopped around on the dock, as they both stared at it in awe. The only thing keeping it from going back into the water was the net it was tangled in.

"You take it off the hook," Eden said as she avoided the flopping creature.

"You caught it; you take it off the hook."

"I'm not touching that thing. What if it bites?" Eden asked as she circled it warily.

"Okay, okay, here's what we'll do. I'll hold its mouth with the pliers. You take the hook out."

"Did you miss the part about it biting me?" Eden said as she backed away.

Jamie put her hands on her hips. "Eden, they don't bite!"

"Then how did it get the hook in its mouth, and why did you ask me if I had a bite earlier?"

"Here, you take the pliers, and I'll get the hook," Jamie huffed in frustration. She wasn't about to let her dinner slip away.

"Again, that puts me at the mouth of the fish!" Eden shot back.

Jamie stomped up to the fish and put her foot on top of it. She snatched the pliers and slowly reached down, dislodging the hook. Lifting up her prize triumphantly, she looked at Eden. "I don't suppose you know how to clean one of these?"

Eden watched the spinner closely as she listened to Jamie squeal in disgust while she attempted to clean their dinner. Eden had landed a good-sized bass. The fish fever had taken hold of her as she waited for her next victim to take a bite.

After a pleasant dinner of broiled bass and biscuits, the two retired to the porch with coffee and pipes, complete with cherry tobacco, which was becoming a tradition for the duration of their stay.

"Do you suppose Holly is somewhere safe?" Eden asked as she stuffed her pipe with the rich-smelling tobacco.

"I hope so," Jamie said with a hint of sadness in her voice. "I hate that we parted on bad terms. I think I let my nerves get the best of me and I took it out on her. She's a resourceful woman, though, and I believe in my heart that she's tucked away somewhere safe and sound."

"What will you do when and if our lives return to normal?" Eden asked.

"Assuming I'm not in prison and I still have my nurse's license, I intend to find another job. Maybe in another clinic."

"You have my word that I'll make sure you have the finest attorneys to represent you if it should come to that." Eden raised her hand to forestall the protest she knew was coming. "It's the least I can do, Jamie."

Jamie bowed her head, slightly embarrassed by the kind gesture. "Thank you," she said softly.

"I've been thinking about hiking a little to boost my energy level, if you think I'm physically ready," Eden said, sensing Jamie's discomfort.

"As long as you don't push yourself too hard when just starting out, I think that would be a great idea."

"Excellent." Eden grinned. "I'll start tomorrow morning."

Mason walked through the empty house, surveying each room to confirm he was indeed alone. Satisfied with his findings, he sat at Paul's desk and opened the humidor, choosing the finest cigar of the lot. He leaned back in the high-backed leather chair, lit the cigar, and blew out the smoke, pleased with his find. Occasionally, he would flick the ashes into the fine rug that surrounded the desk, ignoring the ashtray.

He emptied each drawer and picked through the contents; his anger mounted as he came up with nothing. The answers he sought obviously lay with the owner of the house. He glanced over at the answering machine and for the first time, noticed the flashing red light. He pressed the playback button and relaxed as he listened to the messages.

His scowl deepened as the voices droned on with each message until her heard her voice.

"Paul...I'm getting a little worried that I haven't heard from you. Holly left us today in the van...Please call me as soon as you get this message."

Perhaps it would be worth his time to wait until Paul returned.

Chapter Ten

"Wait up," Jamie called breathlessly as she followed Eden up the trail. "For someone who has been off her feet for a while, you have one hell of a stride."

Eden turned and grinned. "You have yet to see my stamina."

Jamie blushed at the implications of that statement. Her attraction grew for Eden every second of the day, and now that she was no longer considered a patient, Jamie found her feelings of inappropriateness slipping away with the breeze.

"I've noticed your legs; you're not a couch potato, Jamie," Eden called over her shoulder as she resumed her pace.

"Be that as it may, I can't match the stride of your long legs. I'm taking two steps to your one," Jamie answered with a grin, pleased that Eden had taken notice.

Eden paused at the top of a hill and looked out over the lake. "It's so beautiful up here. I can't believe I never bothered to explore what my home state had to offer."

Jamie joined her and rested against a tree. "You were probably cooped up in a stuffy office most of the time."

Eden turned and looked at her for a moment. "You're right, I was. I remember a lot more about where I worked and lived, but I still have a hard time putting two and two together."

"It'll all become very clear to you soon. Just give yourself some time."

"How much time do we have? We're like sitting ducks up here until my memory decides to come home from its holiday."

"No one knows we're here. As you can tell, there's no one around for miles. I think we're as safe as we can be right now." Jamie tried to reassure her, but the same feeling gnawed at her gut.

Al Pittman watched Eden's face as it flashed across his television screen. He hoped that someone would recognize her and call the police, but as the days passed, his hope began to wane. He reached for the phone and dialed the number that he had memorized in the past week.

"Detective Salamoni, have you heard anything yet?"

"No, sir, I'm sorry to say we haven't gotten a response. I haven't given up, though, and all my caseload has been delegated so that I can focus on locating Miss Carlton."

"I know I'm putting a lot of pressure on you, Melanie. I'm sorry," Al replied sadly.

The detective smiled upon hearing him address her so casually. "Never apologize to me, Mr. Pittman. I know you're on pins and needles. I'll call you the minute we hear something."

Detective Salamoni looked at the picture on her desk, smiling at her two children. She could not fathom what it would be like to be in Al Pittman's shoes.

"What's your favorite color?" Jamie asked as they strolled along.

"Black," Eden said with a grin.

"That's not a color."

"Sure it is." Eden chuckled. "I love black cars and black clothes. What's your favorite color?"

"I like green, all shades."

Eden stopped again and grabbed Jamie's arm as she struggled with Donald's old boots. "I'll be so glad to wear my own clothes again," she said as she tugged the boot off and pulled her sock back into place.

Jamie stiffened at the physical contact. Maybe it was being stuck out in the middle of nowhere with an attractive woman, but her libido was kicking in double time. She silently chastised herself for the images that flashed through her mind but still wondered if Eden had any of the same urges.

"This is good, it helps me to remember. Ask me direct questions; it helps to jog my memory," Eden said as she resumed the walk.

Jamie frowned. The brief contact didn't seem to have any effect on Eden. "Well, I know you're pretty much a loner, but don't you have someone in your life you share things with? You know, like a confidant?"

Eden walked along silently, staring at the trail ahead of her. Her mind slowly assimilated the pieces. Peace flooded her being as Al's face appeared in her mind's eye. "Al," she whispered, unaware that she had stopped walking. She turned and looked at Jamie. "His name is Al. If I could contact him, he could get us out of here."

Jamie chewed her lip for a moment, debating whether or not to tell Eden about the hidden cell phone. "Hopefully, when Paul returns, we can give him Al's information, and he can make contact," Jamie offered. She was afraid that Eden would have a weak moment and use the phone to contact someone who might be put in harm's way, or worse—lead someone to their hiding place. "Right now Paul is our only means of communication."

She was ashamed to admit it to herself, but the way Eden spoke of Al so fondly, she wondered what the connection was. "Do you consider yourself bisexual?" she asked suddenly.

Eden stopped in her tracks again and looked at Jamie strangely. "Why would you assume that I was bi?"

Jamie shrugged her shoulders. "You seem to be very fond of this Al person."

Eden chuckled as she resumed her pace. "Al was my grandfather's best friend, and he has filled a big void in my life." Eden stole a quick glance at Jamie. "I'm not bi."

Jamie knew by the way Eden looked at her that her feelings were becoming transparent. A part of her wanted to reveal what she was feeling, but another part was too concerned with making things awkward if Eden didn't feel the same.

Sitting in the coolness of the shade afforded by the small porch, Eden studied Jamie as she rested from their hike. Eden watched the steady rise and fall of her chest as she lay across the porch swing with her head tilted back over the arm rest.

She didn't have to imagine the secrets her clothes held. She had seen all Jamie had to offer the morning of the shower episode. She gulped her water and debated pouring the cold liquid over her head. She could not deny the longing she felt for her touch. And she wondered why Jamie affected her this way.

Was it that she simply wanted a temporary reprieve from the world that she had been thrust into? Was she lonely for companionship because of her situation? Or was it that she simply desired Jamie for who she was? Eden smiled to herself. Who was she kidding? Every time she laid eyes on Jamie, her pulse sped up. The blonde sitting across from her stirred things she hadn't felt in a long time.

"Describe your idea of the perfect mate," Eden said out of the blue, knowingly steering the conversation into more intimate waters.

Jamie lifted her head in surprise. "Where did that come from?" she asked with a chuckle.

"I'm just making conversation. You said my memory would return the more we talked," Eden admitted sheepishly.

"The more we talk about you, not me."

"I can't just sit here and jabber. I have to be inspired to converse, so start talking," Eden responded playfully.

"Perfect mate…Someone intelligent, with a sense of humor. Someone adventurous who likes to do things on the spur of the moment," Jamie replied without looking in Eden's direction, suddenly nervous with the discussion.

"Do looks have anything to do with your choice?"

Jamie ducked her head. "Well, I've always had a thing for brunettes. Blondes really don't appeal to me, but if she had all the qualities I was looking for in a person, I'd make an exception."

"Are you the type to pursue a woman who interests you or are you the more passive type?" Eden asked with a grin.

"I'm actually very shy about that. I usually flirt my ass off until she notices me and makes the first move. How about you?"

Eden grinned. "We have shyness in common. I try to make my feelings known, but it's always very awkward. I seem to do or say the wrong thing."

Jamie watched as Eden squirmed in her seat. "Are you okay? Do you have fleas or something?" Jamie asked with a chuckle.

"No…" Eden's face turned red. "I'm really uncomfortable in these granny panties. I feel like they're up in my ribs."

Jamie threw back her head and laughed. "We're truly roughing it out here, aren't we?"

The soup they shared for dinner paled in comparison to the fish they had the previous night, and they both agreed after their morning hike that they would return to fishing for their meals. Jamie lay on the couch and Eden took the recliner as they watched one of the old movies that Donald had left behind, and Eden repeated verbatim each line of the movie. She was quickly becoming a spaghetti western aficionado.

Eden showered first and retreated to the loft. After Jamie showered and prepared for bed, she eased her way under the covers, careful not to come in contact with Eden, who lay facing the opposite wall.

"Why are you so tense?" Eden asked suddenly, making Jamie jump.

"I'm not tense," Jamie responded defensively.

"You can deny it if you want, but there's a lot of tension between us."

"I think we get along fine," Jamie shot back, knowing well what Eden meant.

Eden rolled over, and it took Jamie a second or two to realize she was being kissed. Her body took over and gave in as she parted her lips and allowed Eden to slip her tongue over her bottom lip.

Eden broke the kiss and rolled back over, facing the wall. "I told you there was tension between us."

"Well, you arrogant ass!" Jamie growled as she yanked the covers back and attempted to climb out of bed. Her escape was thwarted as Eden tugged her back down and covered her body with her own and kissed her again. Jamie struggled for a moment, and again her body overruled her head as she felt herself give in. Eden didn't pull away this time.

Instead she kissed her way across Jamie's cheek and nibbled at her ear, causing what little resistance she had to take flight. Eden's ragged breathing and the insistent grinding of her hips between her thighs caused Jamie's body to shudder uncontrollably.

"Tell me now; do you want me to stop?" Eden whispered into her ear.

"Not now, no," Jamie replied breathlessly as Eden's fingertips trailed over the soft cotton sleep shirt that Jamie wore. Jamie tugged at Eden's shirt, anxious to feel the skin beneath it pressed against hers, as Eden began removing her clothes.

Free of the clothing that kept them apart, Eden lay back down on top of Jamie, who whimpered when hot skin came in contact with hers. She wove her fingers into Eden's hair as Eden again filled her hungry mouth with her tongue.

Spurned on by the steamy kisses and the continuous moans that issued forth from Eden, Jamie flipped Eden onto her back and kissed her way hungrily down Eden's chest, stopping only to take an erect nipple into her mouth. Eden groaned and arched her back as the warm mouth covered her sensitive skin and she felt the tiniest nip of teeth.

Jamie kissed her way farther down Eden's stomach but was stopped when Eden pulled her up until her breasts were just above Eden's face. Eden pulled her close and took the tender flesh into her mouth. Jamie straddled her thigh and began a frantic rhythm. Before Jamie could reach the moment of ecstasy she craved, Eden flipped her onto her back.

"Not yet," she whispered hotly into her ear, as she nibbled the tender lobe. Jamie's body shuddered, and she groaned as the sensations in her body were forced to remain at bay.

"You like to be in control, don't you?" Eden said as she kissed her way down Jamie's body.

Jamie responded by pushing Eden faster down her body. Her stomach quivered as she felt Eden's lips and tongue trail along her skin.

Eden buried her face between Jamie's thighs, causing her to buck uncontrollably. Eden pulled her face away and looked up at Jamie. "Don't get in a hurry for it," she teased. She resumed her ministrations as Jamie clutched the sheets while her breath came in pants.

When Eden's tongue grazed over her most sensitive spot, Jamie's back arched and rose off the bed. "Don't stop now, Eden," she hissed between gritted teeth. An intense and warm sensation spread through her lower body as she gasped a breath and held it. Eden refused to cease her attentions until Jamie gently pushed her away.

Jamie lay in a tangled mass of sweat-covered bed sheets as she regained her strength. Eden still lay between her legs with her head resting on her stomach. "Come here," Jamie said as she tried to tug Eden up her body.

"Give me a minute; I'm too close," Eden said as she tried to pull away.

"Good," Jamie said as she pulled Eden up between her legs and wrapped them around Eden's waist. Eden groaned when she felt the intense heat of Jamie pressed so snugly against her. Jamie pulled Eden roughly to her and slipped her tongue into her mouth as she ground her mound into Eden's.

Eden pulled her mouth away and gasped for breath, as Jamie stilled. "You don't like being teased either, do you?" she said as Eden dug her fingers into the pillow.

Eden lay teetering on the brink, as Jamie ran her nails lightly down her back. She dug her nails into the tender flesh of Eden's backside as she thrust up, rubbing her body against Eden's clit. The combined sensations sent Eden over the edge as she nearly screamed into Jamie's ear.

When Eden's body finally relaxed, Jamie pushed her onto her back. "This time, let me finish what I started," she said as she kissed her way down Eden's sweat-slicked skin.

Jamie awoke to an empty bed. The smell of bacon wafted up to the loft, and her stomach growled in anticipation of breakfast. She pulled on her nightshirt and peered over the railing. She watched as Eden cooked the last of their food.

"Good morning," Jamie chirped as she climbed down from the loft.

Eden said nothing but simply set the cell phone that Paul had given them for emergencies on the table. "I found this tucked away under the hand towels. Why did you lie to me?" Eden demanded. "You said Paul was our only means of communication."

"I was afraid of you getting someone else involved," Jamie said as she ran her fingers nervously through her hair.

"But if we could've gotten help, we'd be out of here by now," Eden countered angrily.

"I simply didn't want you to bring anyone else into this. Have you forgotten about the danger of our situation?"

Eden narrowed her eyes. "What you mean is, you didn't trust me enough to be honest."

"It's not a matter of trust," Jamie reasoned. "I just forgot to tell you about it."

"You forgot to tell me about the gun, and you forgot to tell me about the phone. Is there anything else you forgot to tell me about?"

"Are you implying that I'm intentionally keeping things from you?" Jamie asked, feeling her blood begin to boil.

Eden slammed a plate of bacon down onto the table. "I'm not implying anything. I'm telling you straight out that you've been hiding things from me, and it makes me wonder what your real motives are."

"My motive is simple! I intend for us to stay alive long enough for Donald and Paul to get us out of here safely!" Jamie bellowed.

Eden walked around the table and came face-to-face with Jamie. "Let me get this straight. You took me from the mental health facility and didn't go to the police. You have a phone, but you don't want me to call anyone who might get involved.

Jamie, this sounds a little too suspicious for me," Eden ground out.

"If you think I'm holding you here, then you can march your ass down that dirt road!" Jamie shouted into Eden's face. "As for the phone, use it all you want, then shove it up your ass!" Jamie turned on one heel and stormed into the bathroom.

Eden turned and looked at the phone that still sat on the table, then walked outside to cool off and process what she had learned. In her heart, she wanted to believe Jamie, but circumstances were alarming.

If Jamie was telling the truth, she could endanger Al by calling him. Eden knew the elderly man would ignore his own safety and come looking for her. Doubts niggled at her mind as she walked along the lake.

Jamie stood in the shower, letting the hot spray hit her directly in the face, wanting to wash all traces of Eden from her skin. Eden's mistrust cut her deeply, even after the night they spent together. If Eden did choose to call someone for help, maybe it would mean she would leave this place soon and be free of the woman who tore her heart in two.

Mason drove through the countryside with the windows down, enjoying the crisp autumn air on his skin. He smiled, thinking he was drawing closer to his prey. He could sense their presence.

Susan had been adamant about how he was supposed to carry out his task. He could kill the two nurses any way he saw fit, but Eden was to be made to suffer. A chill ran down his spine as he remembered the look in Susan's eye when she made her request.

"Rape her, beat her, or set her on fire, but make sure death for her comes slowly. I want her to suffer."

Jamie sat on the porch and watched as Eden sat cross-legged on the pier waiting patiently for a fish to bite. Neither of them exchanged a word all morning, and as noon drew near, it looked as though they had reached a stalemate that neither of them was willing to back away from.

As the late afternoon approached, Jamie heard a yelp and ran to the back door of the cabin to see Eden running with a fish in hand and swatting at the air.

"Sorry little bastards!" Eden yelled as she swatted at the wasps that had run her away from the cleaning table.

Jamie chuckled as she walked onto the porch. "Eden, are you allergic to wasps?" she called from the safety of the porch.

Eden looked up at her when she had put distance between herself and the winged tormentors. "No, I'm not!"

"Good," Jamie replied smugly as she turned and went back inside. "Serves you right," she said under her breath.

Eden came back into the cabin shortly after, rubbing her forearms. "Do we have anything for insect stings?"

Jamie glanced up from the book she pretended to read. "There may be something in the bathroom."

Eden stalked off and Jamie could hear cursing as she rummaged through the cabinets.

Eden emerged moments later and dug some ice out of the freezer and held it to her arm. The nurse in Jamie took over, and she fished a small first aid kit out of a drawer. "Let me take a look," she said, tugging at Eden's arm.

"I shouldn't be nice to you after the way you've treated me today," she said as she swabbed at the stings.

"We have a lot to discuss, but I'm still a little angry and I'm afraid of what I may say," Eden said through gritted teeth.

"You're a little angry?" Jamie seethed as she looked up from her task. "You damn near accused me of kidnapping you. I hope whoever you called will bring the police with them so I'll at least have a ride out of here!"

Eden jerked her arm away from Jamie's grasp. "What the hell would you think, Jamie?"

"I would've given you the benefit of the doubt."

"Well, you're not in my shoes, are you?" Eden said as she stomped out of the cabin.

Dinner was tense, to say the least. Both were silent as they ate. Jamie fought the urge to smirk at the red spot just below Eden's right eye and the matching spots on her arms.

When it came time for bed, Eden returned to the couch and Jamie retreated to the loft. She lay alone in the bed they had shared the night before amazed at how quickly Eden had shut her out. She refused to release her anger, knowing when she did the hurt would come, and she would not allow Eden the satisfaction.

Jamie looked at her watch and frowned at the iridescent glow. Midnight and she still had not slept a wink. She didn't understand why she suddenly thought of Donald. Perhaps it was because she was in his cabin, but it seemed as though he was there with her. She rose from the bed and looked out the window. The moon was full and cast pale light over the woods behind the cabin, then she saw it. A dark figure moved along the tree line. She strained her eyes and caught sight of him again as he intentionally avoided the lighted areas.

Hair rose on her arms and along her spine. In her gut, she knew it wasn't Paul or even Donald. She quickly tugged on her pants and crawled down the ladder. Carefully, she placed her hand over Eden's mouth. Eden's eyes snapped open, and she instinctively pawed at the hand until she realized it was Jamie.

"Don't make any noise. Someone's outside and I don't think he wants us to know he's here," she whispered as calmly as she could. Eden nodded, then Jamie withdrew her hand. "Put some pants on," Jamie said as she went to the closet and dug out the gun Paul had given her. She tucked it into the waistband of her pants and dropped to the floor when she saw a shadow pass in front of the cabin.

Eden saw her sudden movement and dropped behind the couch, where Jamie joined her. Eden's eyes moved to the weapon Jamie clutched in her shaking hands. "Do you know how to use that thing?" she whispered.

"Well enough," Jamie replied with a tremble in her voice. "There's only one door. I think he's already tried the windows."

They both quieted as they heard the doorknob being tried. Jamie cocked the handgun and peeked from around the couch.

She jumped as the door blew in off the hinges. Adrenaline took over as she stood and fired the weapon at the figure when it crossed the threshold.

Chapter Eleven

Paul returned home in the early hours of the morning and was stunned to find his back door ajar. He sneaked back to his vehicle and pulled a revolver from the glove compartment before making his way to the door. Slowly, he nudged it open, and the smell of stale cigar smoke filled his nostrils.

He carefully entered the house with the gun held out in front of him. He slid down the wall, keeping his back close to it as his eyes scanned the room for the intruder. When he was certain the house was empty, he surveyed the damage.

His office was nearly decimated. All the drawers had been taken from his desk and emptied in the middle of the floor. Bookshelves had been turned over after their contents had been thrown around the room. Remnants of smoked cigars had been smashed into the carpet.

His kitchen was only slightly cleaner. The refrigerator door had been left open, and the food inside had been gone through. Whoever had been there made it obvious this was not a random break-in.

Paul pulled his cell phone from his pocket and made a call to the emergency phone at the cabin. When he received no answer, he called Donald. When his brother failed to pick up at such an early hour, worry gnawed at Paul's gut. He climbed into the truck and headed toward the cabin.

Jamie ran through the woods in a blind panic with Eden close on her heels. They had not stopped to see if their attacker was dead. Instead they leapt over him and ran for their lives.

Eden grabbed Jamie's shoulder and pulled her to the ground, holding her with her weight. Jamie shook violently beneath her. "I shot that man, Eden. I can't believe I shot someone."

Eden looked into Jamie's wide eyes. "He would've shot us if you hadn't. Right now you've got to get it together because we don't know if he was alone."

Jamie's face blanched at her words.

"There's a car sitting near the road. I can't tell if there's anyone in it," Eden whispered breathlessly.

"Do you think it's his car?"

"Give me the gun," Eden said as she pried the weapon from Jamie's trembling fingers. "I'm going to sneak up and see if it's occupied."

Jamie watched as Eden made her way carefully to the vehicle. Her heart skipped in her chest when she saw Eden step out of the shadows with the weapon raised and approach the old sedan. When Eden waved giving the all clear, Jamie bolted from her hiding place and joined Eden as she circled the car.

"It's his," Eden said grimly as she looked over the things inside. "This is probably how he found us." Eden handed Jamie a utility bill.

"Oh, my God, this is Donald's!" Jamie shrieked.

"Lower your voice," Eden whispered. "As I said before, there may be someone else with him, although by the looks of this car, he came alone. There's trash piled up in all the seats."

"I need to make sure Donald is okay," Jamie said hysterically.

Eden grabbed Jamie by the shoulders. "Look at me," she said sternly. "We've got to go back and get the keys to this car, and I need you to be calm."

Tears glistened in the moonlight as they streamed down Jamie's face. "What if he's not dead?"

"If he's not, he will be soon. You fired off quite a few rounds. I'll get the keys, but I want you to follow me back to the cabin, just on the off chance that there is someone else. I don't feel good about you staying here alone."

Jamie clutched Eden's hand tightly as they crept back toward the cabin, then waited in a cluster of trees as she watched Eden disappear into the darkness just behind the cabin. Never once could she remember being so terrified. The thought of something happening to Eden made her knees weak, causing her to crumble to the ground.

Eden sneaked around the rear of the cabin and came up the side closest to the porch. Each step she made sounded amplified by the crunching of dried leaves under her feet. Every muscle in her body froze stiff as she rounded the corner and looked into a pair of eyes staring back at her eerily in the moonlight.

Paul struggled to remain at a moderate speed as he made his way to the cabin, clutching his cell phone. He had not been able to reach Jamie. He cursed the timing of his sister's illness that kept him away from his older brother and the women who desperately needed his help. He wondered if Donald was not home because he had simply gone to the cabin, but something deep inside told him otherwise.

Eden swallowed hard as she stared into the lifeless eyes of the man who had burst into the cabin earlier. He lay sprawled out on the porch just as he was when they had fled. She willed her feet to move and slowly walked up the steps looking down at the bullet-riddled body.

She nudged him with her foot, and when there was no response, she knelt and carefully went through his pockets. The only sound she made was a sigh of relief when she tugged the key ring free of his pocket. Feeling a little braver, she reached beneath him and pulled out his wallet. Refusing to take the time to peek inside, she stuffed it in her pocket and made her way back to Jamie.

"Where do we go now?" Jamie asked as she sat behind the wheel of the old sedan. Her hands shook violently as she slipped the car into drive.

"Just get us back onto a real road and we'll come up with something then," Eden said as she squinted into the darkness that surrounded them. "I know a place we can go."

Jamie obediently followed Eden's instructions and followed the gravel road until they came to the highway. "What if we're stopped?"

"Don't stop for anyone unless it's the police," Eden said as she fished a cell phone from the trash on the seat. She punched in a number, hoping she had gotten it right.

The sun was barely peeking over the horizon when Paul pulled up in front of the cabin. Tension gnawed at his gut as he slowly crept toward the door, peering over the barrel of his shotgun. The occasional squawk of a bird toyed with his frayed nerves.

In the early morning light, his eyes were barely able to make out the form of a body lying on the front porch. His throat constricted painfully until he was able to ascertain that it was not one of the women he had vowed to protect. Slowly, he stepped over the lifeless man and entered the cabin, his ears straining for any sound.

He began to relax after he found the place was empty. He searched the surrounding area cautiously, calling out for anyone who could hear. After an hour of searching, he reluctantly climbed back into his truck and made his way to Donald's, hoping he would find them alive and well with his brother.

Al Pittman rode in the front seat of the unmarked police car as he and Detective Salamoni intercepted the two women at a meeting spot they had agreed upon. Tears streamed down his face when at last he looked Eden in the eyes. He wasted no time getting out of the car when it came to a stop, and he tugged Eden into his arms.

Jamie watched with tears of her own as the two embraced. She cried tears of joy for them and tears of worry and fear for what may have happened to Donald.

"Miss Spencer, are you all right?" Detective Salamoni asked as she approached the haggard-looking woman.

"Are you going to arrest me now?" Jamie asked nervously.

Detective Salamoni smiled reassuringly. "No, ma'am, as I told you on the phone, we know the truth about what happened.

I'll need you to give a formal statement, but after that, you'll be free to go."

"We just need to eat and to rest, no hospital," Eden stated resolutely as Al tried to convince her to get checked for injuries.

"Can I go home?" Jamie asked the detective.

"You really should be looked at by a doctor," Detective Salamoni tried to argue.

"No hospitals!" Eden demanded.

"Then you'll both come home with me," Al replied staunchly. "They can come home with me, can't they?" he asked the detective.

Detective Salamoni sighed. "Well, if they don't feel they need medical attention, that would probably be best. After I get the report from the sheriff who's working the cabin and this car impounded, I'll need to question them both."

Jamie called her parents from Al's cell phone as they made the trip to his home. Tearfully, she assured them that she was all right. Eden watched her from the backseat, feeling guilty about making the wrong assumptions.

Detective Salamoni and several other members of her team questioned Eden and Jamie until they both looked as though they would drop from exhaustion. Al doted over the two women as they recounted the horrific events since leaving the McManus facility.

During the questioning, Jamie repeatedly asked about Holly, hoping that she had already come forward. Detective Salamoni skirted the issue, fearful that the news would be too much for Jamie in her current state. When Jamie refused to accept another excuse, the detective relayed the information that she dreaded to deliver.

"Miss Spencer, late yesterday evening, we recovered the van that belonged to Beth Briggs. We found signs of a struggle, but we've not been able to locate Miss Patton."

Jamie's heart sank into the pit of her stomach. "What do you mean 'signs'?"

Detective Salamoni sighed. "We found a fair amount of blood that we believe to be Miss Patton's, but the test results haven't come back from the lab."

Jamie shoved away from the table; Eden stood and tried to take her into her arms, but Jamie shrieked and pushed away. Al followed her from the room as Eden stood helpless.

Jamie refused to be consoled until Al convinced her to take some of his medication for anxiety. He stayed with her until she relaxed and her body gave into sleep. The following morning, he was at her door the minute the sun rose.

Al poked his head inside. "May I come in for a second?" He asked politely before stepping into the room. "If there's anything I can get for you, please don't hesitate to ask." He dabbed at his eyes before continuing. "I'll never be able to repay you for what you've done for Eden. She's all I have left in this world."

"There's nothing to repay me for, Mr. Pittman. I'm just thankful you were there for us and I'm not sitting in jail right now," Jamie replied sadly.

"I'll have the lady who tends my home bring up something for you to eat, then I'd like you to try and get some more rest. I'll keep trying to get in touch with Dr. Briggs for you, and if I hear anything at all, I'll wake you myself. Please treat my house as your home." He then backed out of the room, allowing Jamie the rest she so obviously needed.

Later that morning, Eden paced back and forth in the room she had taken refuge in. She jumped when she heard the anguished wail from down the hall. Al had given her the news about Donald Briggs, and she chose to hide while he relayed the same information to Jamie.

She knew it was her place to tell Jamie what had happened to Donald, but the guilt and shame was too great for her. The man who Jamie looked to as a father figure died because of her. And Jamie's life had been turned upside down because she cared enough to help a stranger in need. Eden hid in her room, feeling ashamed and guilty.

146

Chapter Twelve

"I'll have a burger with extra cheese and go heavy on the pickles. I'd also like a large fry and a chocolate shake," Jamie said, looking at the menu of her favorite fast food restaurant.

"Now, that's more like the sister I know and love," Ann said with a smile. "Mom and Dad were really beginning to get worried about your lack of appetite."

Jamie grabbed the tray heavily laden with food and found a table. "I'm fine," she grumbled as she settled into a chair.

Ann decided to keep the conversation light, until Jamie was ready to purge her soul. She would not push her baby sister like her parents had, but she knew something wasn't right. "I imagine you went through some pretty bad junk food withdrawals at the cabin."

Mention of the cabin made the bite of burger sour in Jamie's mouth. She set it down and went to work on her fries. "I won't be in a hurry to have fish or soup anytime soon."

"I wonder if Mom and Dad have made it home yet," Ann wondered aloud as they ate. Their parents spent a month with Jamie until Ann relieved them. Jamie felt smothered by their attention and was close to the boiling point when Ann arrived and assured them that she would be there for her little sister.

"I was pretty hard on them before they left," Jamie said with regret. "They were just in my face all the time wanting to know if I was okay. I just couldn't take it anymore."

"Dad admitted that they had been overbearing. They were so worried about you when you were gone, and I think they expected you to fall apart when you got home."

ROBIN ALEXANDER

"I'm sure that'll happen when I have a moment to myself and I get a chance to think about things. Between our parents, the media, and the police, I haven't been able to go to the bathroom by myself," Jamie said before she realized how she must have sounded. "I…I'm glad you're here, though."

Ann smiled and patted her sister's hand. "I'll give you all the space you need, but I'll be seconds away if you need me."

"I need to call Holly's parents. Detective Salamoni said she would do some research and see if she could get a phone number and address for me…" Jamie's voice went raspy with emotion. "I just wanted to tell them what she meant to me."

After lunch, Jamie took Ann to an older area of town. The ride down tree-lined streets lifted her spirits a little. She smiled as she passed the older homes, thinking this area would soon be her own.

"This is the one," Jamie said as they pulled up in front of the wood-framed house with a wraparound porch.

Ann sighed and paused a moment before getting out of the car. "Jamie, this is a terrible thing to ask, but I need to know. How are you going to afford to buy a house with no job?"

Jamie killed the engine and opened the door, allowing cool air to fill the inside of the car. "Al Pittman is buying it for me. And he won't take no for an answer," Jamie answered guiltily.

"Then why do you sound so ashamed of it?" Ann asked as she took Jamie's hand into her own.

"Because he doesn't owe me a thing, and I feel guilty for getting a reward after what happened to Donald and Holly."

Ann tugged her sister's hand until Jamie looked her in the eye. "They would want you to have this house, you know that. I understand how you must feel, but I'm sure it means a lot to Al to be able to do this for you."

Jamie swallowed hard as she looked across the small lawn to the house of her dreams.

"Is Eden helping with the purchase of this place, too?" Ann asked, watching Jamie flinch at the mention of her name.

"I doubt she knows anything about it," Jamie responded bitterly.

Ann smiled, knowing she had a leg in the door of the conversation she had been dying to have since she arrived. "Let's go give that porch swing a try, and you can tell me all about it."

Jamie smiled weakly at Ann, knowing she had been had. Her sister could always read her like a book. They sat on the swing and chatted about the house until Ann could take it no longer.

"Tell me what really happened with Eden Carlton at the cabin," she blurted out.

"Just like you to get straight to the point," Jamie said with a smile that quickly faded from her face. "I fell in love with her."

"And?" her sister stated impatiently.

"And I have no idea what she feels, if anything at all. She's difficult to read...well, just plain difficult."

"Does she know how you feel?" Ann pressed a little further, testing the waters.

"She has no idea how I feel," Jamie said dejectedly as she remembered how cold Eden was during their last day at the cabin.

"And you're not brave enough to tell her," Ann said, making a clucking noise, which was quickly silenced when Jamie turned angry eyes on her.

"She wouldn't even look at me when we were questioned by the police. Obviously, I was a quick roll in the hay to her."

"You slept with her already?"

"Don't look at me that way, Ann, you slept with Tim on your second date! In the backseat of a Pacer, no less," Jamie exclaimed.

"Touché." Ann held up her hands in defeat. "So you slept with her and now she's clammed up."

"On our last day at the cabin, we got into a vicious fight, and she basically accused me of kidnapping her. And now that she knows the truth, she's made no attempt to apologize or reconcile." Jamie sniffed back the tears. "I have no idea what she thinks of me now."

Ann draped her arm over her baby sister's shoulders. "Honey, I wouldn't rest until I found out. Do you want me to talk to her?"

"I'm not in junior high anymore, Ann, we're a little old for that now," Jamie said ruefully.

"Then you need to do it, Jamie. If for nothing else, simple peace of mind."

"I'm not ready to set myself up for that kind of hurt right now. Maybe when I feel a little better about myself," Jamie said as she stood. "Let's go look in the windows. I want to know what you think of this place."

"Are you sure?" Jamie asked as she set down the box she was getting ready to pack. "Detective, they can't be dead. Holly called someone to pass along a message to them while we were at the cabin. She said they were elderly, and she was worried about them."

"I used Miss Patton's Social Security number to track them down. I'm certain that these people were her parents, and they both passed away within a year of each other five years ago."

Jamie sat down, reeling from the shock. "This doesn't make sense. Maybe she meant an aunt or uncle."

"As far as I can tell, Holly Patton had one brother, and according to him, they've not spoken since their parents died. Apparently, there was a bitter dispute over what their parents left them. He said Holly moved away and hasn't spoken to him since."

"Well, thank you, detective. I'm sorry to have put you through the trouble for nothing," Jamie said sadly before hanging up the phone.

Detective Salamoni switched lines and called another extension. "Carl, hey, it's Melanie. Can you get me the cell phone recovered from the cabin in the Carlton case?" She hung up the phone and smiled. "You're a sly one," she muttered under her breath.

Jamie unpacked the last of her belongings and sighed as she looked around the house she now owned. Significantly larger than her apartment, it paled in comparison to Al's opulent home. She briefly wondered if Eden's house was just as grand.

"She'd probably feel out of place in such a common setting," Jamie said aloud bitterly. She should have been thrilled to be spending the first night in her new home, but the empty feeling she felt inside stole what little happiness she had left.

She plopped down on the sofa and stared out of the huge living room window at the live oak laden with moss that adorned her front yard. She wondered what type of people Eden associated with and if they would snub their noses at her modest home and furnishings.

Now that the nightmare was over, she felt a void in her life. She'd lost her two closest friends and the woman she had foolishly given her heart to. "What will I do now?" she wondered aloud.

A soft knock at her front door interrupted her thoughts. She glanced out the window and smiled when she saw the familiar pickup sitting in her driveway.

"Paul," she said with a grin as she opened the door and fell into his arms. "It's so good to see you again."

"Congratulations on your new home," he said with a smile as he produced a bouquet of flowers. "Give me a tour."

After Jamie led Paul throughout the house, they settled in the den in front of the fireplace. "Have you heard from Eden?" he asked softly.

"Not a peep. I think she's gone on with her life, and I guess it's the way it's supposed to be," Jamie answered sadly as she gazed into the crackling fire.

"I saw her the other day at the courthouse. I hardly recognized her in her own clothes." He chuckled. "I remember seeing her dressed in Donald's old stuff. She didn't speak to me. I guess she just wants to forget everything that happened and go on with life as she knew it."

Jamie sighed. "I suppose I can relate to that."

"That's one of the reasons I wanted to stop by, and I hope I don't churn up a lot of bad feelings by bringing this up." He set a key ring on the table between them. "Those are the keys to Donald's cabin. All the remaining Briggs children wanted you to have it."

Jamie's eyes filled with tears as she picked up the ring.

"I know there were some terrible things that went on there, but you have to admit there were some good ones, too, and I know Donald would've wanted you to have it." He paused and wiped the tears from Jamie's eyes. "I've renovated the whole thing, and I had the satellite hooked back up."

"Paul, I can't accept this," Jamie said, choking back a sob.

"It's yours and the forty-seven acres that surrounds it. If you choose to sell it, that's just fine with us."

Jamie chuckled sadly. "I kind of miss the old place."

"Well, even with the renovations, it's not as nice as your new home, but it'll be a good place to go when you need to retreat," Paul said, hoping that Jamie would accept the gift.

Jamie swallowed the lump in her throat and stared at the fire a long time before she felt composed enough to speak. "I felt so out of place at his funeral. I sat there amongst your family, knowing that my involving him caused his death. I couldn't blame any of you if you despised me, and here you are giving me his cabin."

"I figured you felt that way. It was written all over your face." Paul took Jamie's hand into his own. "My family believes that when it's your time to leave this life, there's nothing anyone can do to alter it. It was Donald's time to go."

Jamie bowed her head as tears slipped down her cheeks. Paul gently tucked his finger under her chin and turned her face so he could look her in the eyes. "You know he wasn't the same after Beth died. He was just going through the motions of living from day to day. Donald is with her now, and I know in my heart he's very happy. You need to let go of the guilt you're harboring."

After he was satisfied that Jamie was okay, Paul prepared to leave. Jamie clutched his hand as she walked him to the door, feeling like a weight had been lifted off her shoulders. Paul was right—Donald was where he had wanted to be for a long time.

"You did know she was at the funeral?" Paul asked as he stepped out the door.

"Who?"

Paul chewed his bottom lip, feeling foolish for letting another cat out of the bag, a habit he seemed to be getting into lately. "Eden. She stood away from everyone, but she was there."

Jamie seemed shocked by the revelation. "Why didn't you say something?"

"She seemed so uncomfortable. I imagine she's been feeling a lot of the same guilt that you have. She probably felt that she didn't belong there, but before I could speak to her, she was gone."

Jamie hadn't considered that Eden may have been feeling guilty, too. "I guess you're right, I'm sure she has some issues of her own."

After Paul left, Jamie took her seat back in front of the fire. Her thoughts were all over the place. She clutched the key to the cabin tightly in her fist and wondered if she would ever have the guts to go back there again. The thought of being there without Eden made her stomach twist into knots.

She thought back on the day when she had planned on dropping in on Al to thank him for all he had done. She parked on the street but hesitated getting out of her vehicle when a sports car pulled into the drive. The woman who stepped out was a far cry from what she had seen before.

She stared open-mouthed as she watched the tall figure emerge from the car. Even from a distance, Eden looked so regal in her business suit and long overcoat. Unconsciously, Jamie's fingers clutched the steering wheel as she remembered what it was like to run her fingers through the brown hair that now hung well past Eden's shoulders.

ROBIN ALEXANDER

Chapter Thirteen

Eden ran her fingers through her hair as she stared at the phone number Al had scrawled on a piece of paper. Her hand trembled as she reached for the phone.

"I have the reports you asked for, Miss Carlton," Charlotte Miller, her new personal assistant, said as she walked into the office.

Eden snatched her hand away from the phone and regarded the elderly woman who stood before her desk. "Thank you, Mrs. Miller. Do you have a minute?"

"Of course," Charlotte replied. "Will I need my notebook?"

Eden smiled. "No, ma'am, this is more of a personal nature. Please have a seat."

Charlotte sat and waited expectantly for Eden, who seemed to be struggling with what she wanted to say.

"I've…deeply wounded someone with a wrong assumption, and I'm not sure how to make amends."

Charlotte smiled. She was touched that her young boss had chosen her for advice. "Have you tried simply apologizing?"

"It's been a while since we've spoken, and I'm afraid too much time has passed." Eden sighed. "I'm afraid she's written me off."

"Miss Carlton, the longer you put things like this off, the more the wound festers and it becomes harder for the other person to forgive. You need to at least make an attempt."

"I knew you'd say that," Eden said with a wry grin. "I'm just going to have to face the music."

"It'll be worth it, if you can mend the friendship that obviously means so much to you," Charlotte said as she stood and prepared to leave Eden to her task.

"Thank you for your time, Mrs. Miller, and in the future, please call me Eden. I feel a little funny having you address me so formally."

"Please feel free to call me Charlotte, and if you need a shoulder to lean on, you can reach me anytime day or night. You have my home number."

"Thank you, Charlotte, that means a lot," Eden said, feeling her stomach clench again as she glanced down at Jamie's number. Not only had time passed since their fight at the cabin, but Eden still harbored guilt over the deaths of Donald and Holly. A simple apology didn't seem to be enough.

"I love painting, it's so therapeutic," Jamie said as she dipped her brush into the hunter green paint and brushed it over one of the shutters on her new home.

"Well, chipping and sanding downright sucks," Ann huffed as she wiped the sweat from her brow. "You know, there are people who do this for a living. They're called professional painters, you can find them in the phone book."

"I'm saving a lot of money by doing this myself, and remember, you volunteered." Jamie playfully flicked paint at her sister.

"I know it makes you uncomfortable to hear this, but I'm more than happy to give you all the money you need until you get back on your feet." Ann held up her hand to forestall the protest. "You can pay me back by babysitting for a weekend or two. That in itself is worth a fortune to me."

Jamie continued to paint one long stroke after another. "I have enough money to get me through the next few months. I just don't want to deplete my savings. And I do have a few job prospects lined up, I just need a break before returning to the workplace."

Ann reached up and grabbed her sister's arm gently. "Look at me, Jamie. Don't go back to work until you're absolutely ready. You've been through a lot and you still need time to heal. I'm more than willing and able to support you until that time."

Jamie grinned at Ann. "You love me, don't you?"

"Love you? I don't even like you. Life was great until Mom and Dad decided to bring you into the world," Ann said with a chuckle.

"No, you love me! I can see it in your eyes," Jamie teased as she pulled her sister into her arms.

"Get off of me, you freak," Ann protested jovially.

"Not until you say you love me." Jamie hugged tighter.

"Just because I'm older now doesn't mean I can't still whip your ass," Ann said, shrugging out of the hold and dropping Jamie to the ground. "How'd you like some grass for lunch?" Ann said with a menacing grin as she sat on Jamie, pinning her to the ground while dangling a handful of grass and soil above her face.

"Am I interrupting something?" Eden asked, surprising the two women who did not hear her approach.

Ann looked up at the tall brunette speechless, as Jamie spit and sputtered against the soil raining down onto her face.

"I was hoping you'd have a minute to talk," Eden said to Jamie as she stood there awkwardly with her hands clasped behind her back.

Ann got up and pulled Jamie to her feet. "I'll go inside and make myself useful," she said before scampering off.

Jamie brushed at the dirt on her face. "How did you find me?"

"Al gave me your address. It's a nice place you have here," Eden offered as she looked around.

"Well, I'm sure it's not what you're accustomed to, but for me, it's perfect," Jamie responded with an edge in her voice.

Eden cocked a brow. "Are you implying that it's too simple for my taste?"

Hurt and anger bubbled to the surface, and Jamie felt no urge to control her emotions. "Why are you here, Eden?"

Taken aback by the hostility in Jamie's voice, Eden took a deep breath and steeled her nerves. "I came to apologize for the way I acted back at the cabin."

"Took you a while, didn't it?" Jamie seethed. "Did Detective Salamoni finally convince you of my innocence?"

"Jamie, I knew you were trying to help me, but that last day when I found that phone, I was shocked and I overreacted. I couldn't understand why you kept it from me."

"You should've given me the benefit of the doubt!" Jamie shouted. "I lost two friends trying to help you and you turned your back on me!"

The hurtful words slammed into Eden, leaving her stunned for a moment. "This was a bad idea. Have a nice life, Jamie," Eden said as she pulled an envelope from her coat. "I hope this helps you." She held it out to Jamie.

Jamie snatched it from her hand and looked at the check inside as Eden walked toward her car.

"You have the audacity to think money would make everything all right?" Jamie yelled as she followed Eden to her car. "Is that how you solve your problems? Just throw a wad of money at it? You really are a rich brat!"

Eden spun on one heel and came nose to nose with Jamie. "That money was for you to furnish your new house that *I* bought, not Al. I knew if he told you the truth, you wouldn't take it. I felt it was the least I could do for you!" Eden watched as Jamie's face flushed even redder with anger.

"And you're right—I do have a lot of money, but aside from Al, that's all I have. You have a family who obviously adores you, and that makes you far richer than I could ever be!" Eden shouted into Jamie's face.

"You're right. Had I known it was you behind the purchase of this house, I would've never taken it. I don't want anything from you," Jamie replied in a calm but cold tone.

"Well, now you're stuck with it." Eden tugged the door to her car open and climbed inside, hearing the muffled curses that Jamie spewed.

"Don't you think you were a little harsh?" Ann asked as Jamie stormed into the house.

"I'm sure you listened to every last word, too," Jamie sneered.

"Yep, and Mom would fall over dead if she heard what you yelled when Eden drove away."

"I'm not in the mood to discuss this," Jamie said as she plopped down on the couch.

Ann ignored the comment. "She didn't deserve that, she was trying to apologize."

"Don't push me, Ann."

"Why? Are going to go all ape shit on me like you just did in your own front yard?"

"I think it's time for you to go home," Jamie growled.

Ann sat in the chair opposite Jamie. "I think seeing her again brought all the pain to the surface." Ann paused for a second as Jamie glared at her. "I think that explosion was coming for a while now, and she just happened to light the fuse."

"Did you sneak off and get a psychology degree?" Jamie asked sarcastically.

"No, and it doesn't take one to know what just happened. Jamie, it wasn't her fault what happened to Donald and Holly, and you know this, but in some small way, I think you blame her."

"I know it's not her fault," Jamie said quietly. "It's mine. There were so many things I could've done differently. I should've been patient, but I had to have the answers I wanted immediately." Tears streamed down Jamie's face. "I'm angry at myself."

"In hindsight, everything is so simple. We all go through life thinking how much better it would be if only we had done some things differently."

"Yes, but the consequences of my decisions were so severe. Sometimes I can hardly bear the guilt," Jamie said as she rubbed her eyes.

"You do realize that Eden feels a lot of the same guilt, and that probably explains why it took so long for her to face you."

"And I ripped her to shreds," Jamie said sadly.

"The ball is in your court now, little sister, but I strongly suggest you take some time to get yourself together before you approach her," Ann said as she took a seat next to Jamie. "I'll be here for you to yell and scream at for as long as it takes."

Jamie looked up and smiled. "You do love me, admit it."

Eden pulled into Al's driveway and found him sitting outside in the sun.

"Beautiful day, isn't it?" he said cheerfully as Eden approached.

"Actually, this day sucks in a major way." Eden took a seat next to him.

"You look as though you've been crying. What's wrong, love?" he asked, taking her hand.

"I went to see Jamie today, and she told me to be fruitful and multiply but not in those words."

Al arched his gray brows. "What does that mean?"

"She told me to screw off, that was the censored version," Eden said as she stared at the ground.

Al chuckled. "I don't mean to laugh, darling, but that child is a little spitfire, isn't she?"

"Yes, and she reduced me to a pile of ashes," Eden replied sadly.

"She's dealing with a lot, just as you are. Give her some space and you'll be able to patch things up."

"She'll have all the space she needs because I'm not going to try that again."

"You two need each other after going through so much together, don't be so quick to give up. True friendship is worth the wait."

Eden sat quietly kicking at the grass.

"Is there something you'd like to tell me?" Al asked softly.

Eden took a breath. "No, sir. I'm just going to go home and mull things over."

"Very well then, but you know I'm here whenever you want to talk. You know you can bare your soul to me with no condemnation," Al said as Eden rose from her seat.

Eden leaned over and kissed him on the cheek. "I know and I love you for it."

Al watched as she walked back to her car, shaking his head at the stoic woman. She was more like her grandfather than she realized. It was like pulling teeth from the elder Carlton to get him to talk about things that troubled him, and Eden was no different. He left the door wide open for Eden to confirm his suspicions about the relationship he suspected she and Jamie had. He wanted to comfort her, but he would not push, at least not this day.

"Rich brat," Eden hissed under her breath. She knew she should have just gone home, but instead she found herself cruising down the tree-lined street that led to Jamie's house. She pulled in behind a car parked on the street and watched as Jamie and the woman who was obviously her sister backed out of the driveway.

The woman was only an inch or two taller, but her and Jamie's facial features were too similar not to be closely related.

"Where are we going?" Jamie asked grumpily as Ann pulled onto the main road.

"We're going to get something to eat, then go shopping."

Jamie scowled. "I'm not in the mood for shopping today, Ann."

"Well, I'm not in the mood to eat pizza for every meal like we've had for the past two days. You need food in your house, and a bag of Oreos and soda do not count."

"I don't cook," Jamie said as she reached for the volume on the stereo. "Don't you have anything other than KC and The Sunshine Band?"

"You can cook, you just don't like to. And don't knock my music, it's much better than that rap crap you listen to. That's the way I like it, uh-huh, uh-huh," Ann sang along with her favorite band.

"You really shouldn't sing, animals are falling dead in the street," Jamie said as she rubbed her temples. "Somebody please put me out of my misery."

"Would a rich brat paint your house?" Eden said aloud as she looked proudly at the freshly painted shutters. Jamie had neglected to pick up the remnants of her painting job, and Eden found the task too tempting. "Now for my signature," she said with a grin as she strolled to the back of the house.

"I just love sliding glass doors," she said under her breath as she dipped the brush into the bucket.

The following morning, Jamie arose to the sound of Ann's laughter. She dragged herself out of bed and was fastening her robe when Ann met her in the hallway. "I've got good news and bad," she said much too cheerfully.

"Give me the bad news first," Jamie said as she rubbed the sleep from her eyes.

"Nope, the good news first—the shutters are painted," Ann said with a grin.

"You painted already this morning?" Jamie asked groggily.

"No, she did," Ann said, stepping out of Jamie's view of the glass door.

Compliments of the rich brat was scrawled across the glass door in green paint. "Son of a bitch!" Jamie hissed as she stared at the sight.

"It was dark when we got in last night, I didn't notice it until now," Ann said with a giggle. "At least she rinsed the brushes out."

"I don't know whether to be happy she painted the shutters or pissed off that I'll have to spend my Sunday scraping paint off the glass," Jamie said between clenched teeth.

"Look at the bright side—she did a wonderful job on the shutters," Ann tossed in as she slipped into the bathroom.

Eden puttered around her house, looking for something to keep her hands busy and her mind on something other than Jamie. Still emotionally bruised from the day before, she was determined to go on with her life and leave Jamie to hers. She tried not to remember how cute Jamie looked with sprinkles of dirt on her face or how her blonde hair glowed in the fading sunlight as she stood on the curb cursing like a sailor.

She thought back on how Jamie had been there for her and began to feel guilty for her childish prank. "Flowers say it best," she said as she pulled the phone book out and searched for a florist.

Thinking they would mean more by being personally delivered, Eden walked slowly up Jamie's driveway with the bouquet of carefully chosen flowers. Her hands shook with nervous anticipation as she knocked on the door. When no answer came, she breathed a sigh of relief until she heard voices coming from the backyard.

Rounding the corner of the house, she paused and listened to the playful banter between sisters. All the ugliness from the day before faded away, and the sight of Jamie in an old pair of jeans and sweatshirt filled her with a longing to hold the feisty blonde in her arms. She clutched the flowers even tighter and slowly made her way toward the two women.

Ann was the first to notice her. "Hi, Eden," she said cheerfully.

Jamie was taken by surprise and was emotionally unprepared to face Eden again so soon. Her defense mechanisms kicked in before she could gain control. "What are you doing here, Eden?" she snapped.

"I came to apologize for this." She pointed to her handiwork. "I was hoping you might be in a better mood so we could talk."

"You painted my glass door and thought it would put me in a better mood?" Jamie screeched.

Ann cringed as she watched the exchange.

"I said I was sorry," Eden ground out as she thrust the flowers into Jamie's hand.

Jamie glanced down at the flowers, and for a split second, it looked as though Eden was getting through to her, but then she made a move that surprised Eden and Ann. She ripped a hand full of blooms off the bouqet and let the petals drop onto Eden's boots. "That's what I think of your apology," she hissed as she turned and marched back into the house, unceremoniously dropping the rest of the bouquet to the ground.

Eden looked down at her feet. "I can't believe she did that," she said in a bewildered tone.

Ann fought the urge to giggle. "I'm sorry, Eden. She's been a horse's ass for a while now. Would you mind sitting down for a minute?" she asked as she brushed a few leaves off the seat next to her.

Eden sank into the chair, her gaze still fixed on the toe of her boot.

"I've been trying to get her to see someone professionally to help her work through this, but she's as stubborn as an ox," Ann said. "She has terrible nightmares about shooting that man at the cabin, and the guilt over Donald and Holly has really been working her nerves. When she sees you, it makes it all real again, and she reacts like this."

Eden sighed. "Well, she won't have to worry about seeing me anymore. This has been hard on me, too, and I can't keep putting myself through this. I told myself yesterday that I wouldn't come here again, but here I am like a pathetic dumbass."

"Don't give up so easily, sweetie. Just give it a little time."

"I thought I had given her time, and she wasn't happy with that either," Eden said angrily as she stood. "I can't seem to please her, no matter what I do."

"She's been a grade A asshole, but she's crazy about you, Eden. Just let her work through this and I'm sure she'll be a different woman," Ann pleaded as she followed Eden around the house.

"Well, when she gets back to normal, tell her to give me a call." Eden jerked the door to her car open.

Ann grabbed Eden by the shoulder and gently halted her. "I'm Ann, her sister, by the way," she said with a smile as she extended her hand.

Eden sighed and did her best to calm down. "I'm Eden, and it's nice to meet you, even under the circumstances," she said as she shook Ann's hand.

"Welcome to the family, Eden," Ann said with a grin.

Eden chuckled. "I see insanity runs in the family."

"No, I just have faith that I'll be seeing you for a long time to come. I bet by the holidays you'll be at my parents' house with the rest of the Spencer clan."

"You've got enough faith for the both of us," Eden said with a wry grin as she climbed into her car.

"Well, you really screwed the pooch this time," Ann said when she walked into the house.

"Lay off, Ann," Jamie growled. "You were the one who said I needed time, so give it to me!"

"I'll give you all the time you need, and I'll be here when you need to talk. Eden, however, will not. She's not coming back, so you win," Ann said as she made her way to the kitchen.

Jamie clamped her eyes shut and curled into a ball on the couch. Ann's words cut her to the core, and she felt powerless to control her emotions. The one thing she wanted most in the world was to have Eden in her life, but whenever she saw her, something angry took over.

The memory of the hurt expression on Eden's face made her stomach turn.

Chapter Fourteen

Al Pittman hugged Eden and reveled at how good it was to have her in his arms. He had cherished every moment since her return like it was the last. However, Eden's visits had been few over the past month, and Al worried about the amount of time she spent alone.

"Grace will have dinner out shortly," he said as he poured Eden and himself a glass of wine. "I'm sorry to tell you that I still haven't been able to track the money Laura pilfered from your accounts. She's a crafty devil, I have to give her that." He took a seat across from Eden.

"Don't waste any more of your time on that, Al, the money is not important to me," Eden responded flatly.

"What else do I have to do? My dearest girl won't entertain me," he shot back playfully.

"I'm sorry, Al. I haven't felt like visiting much lately."

"Eden…" he began, when she interrupted him.

"Please, Al, let me sort this out on my own."

Grace set dinner on the table, and they sat down to eat. Al watched as Eden picked at the food on her plate, taking only an occasional bite.

Undaunted by Eden's refusal to discuss anything regarding the past events, Al forged ahead carefully. "I had a visitor the other day."

Eden grinned and looked up from her plate. "Was it that widow who has had her sights set on you lately?"

Carol is a very interesting lady, I plan to take her to dinner tomorrow evening, but that wasn't whom I was referring to.

Jamie came by, and we had a really nice talk." Al watched as Eden paused from taking a sip of her drink, but her eyes never met his.

"She told me Dr. Briggs's family gave her the old cabin, and she's planning on going up there this weekend. Such a kind thing they did for her, but I hate to see that child return there alone." Al paused, waiting for a reaction.

Eden continued to toy with her meal, avoiding his gaze. "Since you feel so strongly about this, why don't you accompany her yourself?"

Al fought the urge to smirk. "Because, my love, that would be your place."

"We've been over this before; I have no desire to have this conversation."

Al set down his silverware and took a sip of wine. "Yes, we have been over this before, and I honored your request, but now I believe it's time we talk."

Eden dropped her fork loudly onto the plate in front of her. "I think it's time for me to go home."

"I insist you remain right where you are, Eden Carlton." Al never raised his voice and his tone brooked no argument.

Eden's jaw sagged in surprise at the firm command. Al had never taken such a stance with her, but then again, she'd never put him in a position to have to.

"Now that you've ruined my appetite, you'll accompany me to my office." Al stood and Eden dutifully followed.

Al poured them both a brandy and motioned for Eden to take the chair opposite his. "I didn't think it was possible, but you're even more stubborn than your grandfather. The only difference is he never gave up."

Eden didn't answer but instead looked out the window into the darkness.

"I know about the affair you had with Laura McManus." He watched as Eden's posture stiffened. "And I can only assume by your behavior that something occurred between you and Jamie. The child nearly burst into tears when she looked at your picture the other day."

Eden bowed her head, and he watched as the first trickle of tears streamed down her cheek.

Al softened his tone. "If you're afraid that I'm going to disapprove or condemn you for it, you're wrong. What I do disapprove of is you running away and refusing to deal with something that had such an effect on you."

Eden fought to contain her emotions, and tears streamed unbidden down her face. "If you were in her shoes and lost two of your closest friends because of me, wouldn't I be a constant reminder of that?"

"You were no more the cause of their deaths than she was. The circumstances surrounding what happened are what they are, and nothing can change that. Eden, you can't die right along with them."

"She has made it implicitly clear that she wants nothing to do with me. Apparently, I remind her of too much," Eden said as she stood and began to pace around the room.

"She does care, that much was obvious during our visit the other day. And she admitted her regret over being so hostile to you."

Eden sank wearily into the chair. "I'm not sure I want to set myself up for that kind of rejection again, Al."

"Eden, she came here to tell me she was going up to the cabin alone, she all but asked me to let you know. She's extending an invitation."

"Then why didn't she simply pick up the phone and give me a call?"

Al took a sip of his brandy. "I suppose she was afraid she would get the hell she's been giving you."

Eden looked away. "How long have you known about Laura and me?"

"I found out during the investigation. I would've preferred to hear it from you, but I understand why you were reluctant to tell me," Al said softly.

"I didn't want to disappoint you."

"I want only to see you happy and with someone who truly loves you for who you are, not your holdings, and I believe Jamie does truly love you."

"What if you're wrong? What if I get out to the cabin and she says she just wants to be friends?"

"I'm never wrong," Al said adamantly.

Eden did look at him then with a raised eyebrow.

Al chuckled. "I'm a good judge of character, and this old man has great instincts. That woman loves you. Go to her."

Chapter Fifteen

Detective Salamoni regarded the inmate coolly as she was led into the room and placed in a seat opposite the table where she sat. "I'm not going to sit here and mince words with you, Ms. McManus. The evidence against you is damning, and you're going to serve a very long sentence. There's no need to protect her," the detective said before taking a sip of her coffee.

Laura sat with a twisted smile on her face. "Am I to sit here and pretend I know who you're talking about?"

Detective Salamoni set the cell phone on the table sealed in a plastic bag marked evidence. "I know she called you—your number is on this phone."

"I have no idea who you're talking about," Laura replied calmly. Her father had always gotten her out of a jam, and this time would be no different. There was no way she would admit to anything, nor did she plan on spending the rest of her life in a cage.

Detective Salamoni had seen this type of behavior many times before, and years of experience kicked in. "You may think you're untouchable because of your family's wealth, but money and smooth-talking lawyers can only go so far when you're guilty." The detective fought the urge to smile when she saw tension fill Laura's face.

"And everyone affiliated with this case can smell the guilt that surrounds you. That's exactly why you were denied bail for trying to leave the country."

"I look forward to the day when that smug look falls off your face and I walk out of here a free woman," Laura said with controlled anger.

Detective Salamoni did laugh at that. "Your father has agreed to cooperate with us, Ms. McManus. The only place you'll be walking is back and forth from your cell." The detective watched as Laura visibly shook, trying to control her rage.

"My dad used to always tell me, regardless of a person's station in life, we're all just people capable of all kinds of things good and bad. I've never found that statement truer than when I look at you. Ms. McManus, you are trash and a murderer, no amount of money will ever change that."

Detective Salamoni rose from her seat, with her eyes locked on Laura's cold face. "Whether you come to your senses or not, I'll find her."

Jamie felt tension climb up the back of her neck as she turned onto the gravel road leading to the cabin. Memories of her first trip there were still fresh in her mind. It was ironic how the same anxiety plagued her now as it did that evening that seemed so long ago.

As the cabin came into view, sadness and longing overtook the anxiety. Without conscious thought, her foot moved to the brake, and she debated turning around and leaving it all behind. Choking down the last bit of her resolve, she finished the short drive and got out of her vehicle before she lost her nerve.

Jamie ran up the steps, knowing that if she didn't do it quickly, she would never cross the threshold. The old planking on the porch had been replaced, and a new door greeted her as she stood gathering her courage.

With a twist of the shiny brass key, the door opened and Jamie took a tentative step inside. Pushing the tidal surge of memories aside, she concentrated on the changes that Paul had made. New appliances sat in the kitchen waiting to be used, but the old table she used to sit at was still there. She ran her fingertips lightly over the marred surface, thinking of all the conversations shared there. She could hear Holly's laughter echo in her mind.

The old couch and recliner had been replaced with new pieces. Paul had chosen a rustic-looking fabric that matched the mood of the cabin. A new coffee table had been added to the mix, and on it sat a remote for the satellite system, which brought a smile to Jamie's face.

Avoiding the loft, she chose to check out the bathroom that remained exactly the same. Images of being alone in that tiny room with Eden played across Jamie's mind, causing her to slam the door behind her. She circled the ladder to the loft knowing that she would have to go up there eventually.

As she ascended the ladder, a sliver of disappointment washed over her as she noticed that it was exactly as it had been before. Part of her wished that Paul had replaced the bed that she and Eden had shared, helping to erase the memories.

"I need a pack of cigarettes, please."

"What brand?" the heavy-set woman behind the counter asked.

Eden thought for a minute. "I'm not really sure, I don't smoke…well, I mean, I do today," she said, looking sheepishly at the clerk.

An amused smile spread slowly across the woman's face. "Need something to calm your nerves?"

"Yes, and I don't believe in drinking and driving, so I'll have to settle for this."

The clerk chuckled. "Okay then, you have a decision to make. Do you want menthol or regular?"

"Regular, I think." Eden looked at the lighters, and the choices were slim. She chose the half-naked woman over the rebel flag.

The clerk rang up her purchases and stuffed the cigarettes, a pack of gum, and the naked lady lighter into the bag. She smiled at Eden as she handed it over the counter. "I wish you luck with whatever you're facing."

Eden laughed nervously. "Thank you, I need all the help I can get."

With a little practice, Eden managed to shift her car and smoke the cigarette that made her gag and cough. The only consolation was the mild high the nicotine gave her. She puttered along at seventy miles per hour as the rest of the interstate traffic sped by her.

She'd never driven any less than ten miles over the posted speed limit on the highway since first getting her driver's license. Today, however, she was in no hurry, but drove along lost deep in thought. The urge to turn around had been so strong that she exited the interstate several times, only to pull back on minutes later.

In her career, Eden had made many tough decisions, but this was the toughest by far. With work, she would study the pros and cons and spend countless hours going over different scenarios of what the outcome might be. But with Jamie, she was clueless and felt a vulnerability that she had rarely felt before. Feeling as though her life depended on how Jamie would receive her kept her on the plotted course.

Wrapped in a blanket on the porch swing, Jamie watched as the sun set over the lake like she had so many times before. The peacefulness of her once-safe haven was overshadowed by a loneliness that she knew she could no longer tolerate. When Eden didn't show, she resigned herself to the fact that this place would no longer be a comfort to her. The next day at first light, she would pack up and go home. A single tear slid down her cheek as she thought of ways to tell Paul that she could not keep his gift.

When the last rays of sun faded into the darkness, Jamie left her perch and settled on the couch, looking for something on television to take her mind off Eden and the memories that haunted her. But memories returned to her one by one, leaving her in tears again. "Why did I ever do this to myself?" she wondered aloud. "I should've accepted her apology when it was offered."

She awoke the following morning on the couch, relieved to see the sun pouring in through the windows and pleased with herself for spending the night in the place that often haunted her dreams. She walked groggily into the bathroom and went through her morning routine before giving the cabin one last look.

As she made her way down the porch steps, she looked out at the lake and the pier that jutted out into the serene waters. Feeling that she couldn't close the book on this place without walking across those wooden planks, she strolled to the water's edge.

A crisp wind blew in off the water, penetrating the thick layer of clothing that Jamie wore. She closed her eyes and listened to the gentle lapping of the water against the pier, and in her mind, she heard Eden's laughter. She turned to make her way back up the hill before her emotions got the better of her when she saw the sports car pull to a stop.

Eden had arrived at the cabin in the middle of the night, but when the memory of Jamie filling their intended assassin with bullets came to mind, she resisted knocking on the door. Instead she found a spot up the road where she sat until morning, smoking cigarettes and drinking coffee from a thermos, still trying to gather her nerve.

Her heart pounded in her chest as she watched Jamie turn and look at her car. Summoning all the courage she had left, she climbed out of the car and made her way slowly down to the pier. All the speeches she had rehearsed in the wee hours of the morning fled with the breeze.

"Um...hi...Al told me you'd be here," Eden said as she approached warily.

Jamie looked at her as though she were a ghost. Eden stood before her wearing jeans, boots, and a V-neck sweater covered by a brown leather jacket. It struck Jamie funny that even though she had seen Eden a few times, she never realized how good she looked in her own clothes. "You stink. Have you been in a bar all night?" Jamie asked as she kept her distance.

Eden expected a number of responses but not to be told she smelled bad. That was plain insulting. "I smoked some cigarettes on the way up here."

"Some? You smell like you've smoked a whole pack."

Eden shrugged. "Actually, I did, and when I ran out, I bought a carton."

"So did you come here to see me, or did you miss this place?" Jamie asked, not knowing to say.

"Actually, I had an undeniable craving for fresh fish," Eden said as she shuffled nervously from one foot to the other. "And I was hoping you would be willing to talk to me now."

"What's on your mind?" Jamie asked meekly.

"Can we go inside? Your teeth are chattering."

"I'm not cold, I'm nervous," Jamie said as she awkwardly approached Eden, wanting to hug her.

Unsure of Jamie's intentions after their last two meetings, Eden stepped back and lost her footing, sending her headlong into the lake.

"Can you swim?" Jamie called out while looking for something to help Eden, as she struggled under the weight of her clothes to make it to the bank.

"Unfortunately for you!" Eden barked as she grasped at the slick reeds.

Jamie couldn't help herself and laughed hysterically as Eden scrambled up the bank. "I didn't push you, you stepped off the dock."

Soaked to the bone and feeling slightly hypothermic, Eden stomped back onto the pier. "I had no way of knowing what you would do after the last time I saw you. For all I know, you were coming to claw my eyes out!"

Jamie put her hands up in surrender. "I'm sorry. I know I was an asshole, but I promise to behave now. I really need to talk to you."

"I drove all night and slept in the woods until daylight so we could do just that, but if you're going to tell me that we just need to be friends, say it now so I can change my clothes and get out of here," Eden said as her teeth chattered against the cold.

"I promise that's not what I'm going to say. How about you go in and take a shower before you freeze to death?" Jamie said as she slowly approached Eden again.

Jamie was still chuckling at Eden's mishap as she made the coffee. When she heard the water in the bathroom shut off, she quickly poured Eden and herself a cup, then sat at the table, nervously awaiting Eden's return.

Eden emerged minutes later with her wet hair combed away from her face, wearing jeans and a sweater that she brought with her.

"It's a good thing I made a fire this morning or you would be frozen stiff," Jamie said, sliding the hot cup of coffee in front of Eden as she sat.

"Does this have rat poison in it or something that'll make me shit for a week?" Eden asked sarcastically as she eyed the cup.

"Neither, it's a peace offering. I'm sorry about the way I've acted and you falling into the lake," Jamie offered.

Eden nodded and took a trusting sip, enjoying the way it warmed her still-frozen core. "I'm sure I deserved it after the way I've behaved," Eden acquiesced. She nervously tucked her wet hair behind her ear. "I should've contacted you right after we got home, but I felt so guilty for your loss. I felt like you might've needed a break."

Jamie opened her mouth to speak, but Eden held up her hand.

"I don't know how to say this other than just laying my feelings out on the table. I regret how we left things the last day we spent here alone." Eden watched Jamie's face for signs that she wanted to hear what she had to say. Jamie avoided her eyes but drummed her fingers on the table. Eden took comfort in the fact that Jamie seemed as nervous as she was.

"The night we spent together meant more to me than I was willing to admit to you or even myself. One night at dinner, you made the comment that you migrated to people who weren't looking for serious relationships. That comment played through my mind over and over, and I was so afraid that you were going to tell me that what we shared would only remain while we were stuck out here. Then when I found the phone, I allowed my anger to take over."

"I don't…" Jamie tried to interject, but Eden stopped her again.

"Wait, please. I need to get this off my chest before I lose my nerve.

"The morning when Detective Salamoni told us about Holly, I tried to comfort you, but you pushed me away. I tried to convince myself that you didn't want me anymore. Plus I felt so responsible for her and Donald's death that the guilt was more than I could bear." Eden's eyes brimmed with tears. "Some days, it's almost too much for me to cope with."

"I understand how you feel," Jamie said, as her voice filled with emotion. "I've been struggling with my own guilt. That's why I was such a jerk."

"Jamie, I never meant to hurt you. I've questioned my feelings for you every minute of every day. I needed to be sure that it wasn't feelings of indebtedness that makes me feel the way I do about you."

"And how is it that you feel about me?" Jamie asked, meeting Eden's eyes for the first time.

Eden's face flushed with color. "I thought my attraction to you was because you took such good care of me, but I think the day I hooked you with the fishing lure on the lake, I lost my heart. I just was so afraid to let go and tell you how I felt."

Jamie's mind reeled from the words Eden spoke. "I…I was so caught up in my feelings of rejection and guilt over what happened that it never occurred to me what you may have been going through," Jamie stammered. "And when we got home and you pulled away from me, I just lost it."

"I guess my lack of fortitude kept us from being there for each other in an extremely difficult time, but if you'll forgive me, I promise to never let that happen again."

"Are you saying you want another chance…with me? Even after the way I behaved?" Jamie asked shyly.

Eden tentatively reached across the table and took Jamie's hand. "I would love to know where things will go with us. And thanks to Ann, I understand why you wanted to rip my head off there for a while."

"Well, you're not the only one who lost her heart," Jamie said with a chuckle. "I could've told you how I felt, too. I think I fell for you the day I shaved your legs."

"Nothing spells romance like a woman's hairy legs," Eden teased. "You can shave my legs every anniversary."

"Do you believe we'll celebrate anniversaries?"

"Till we're old and gray," Eden said with a grin.

Jamie's expression turned serious. "You were right that morning; we come from two very different backgrounds."

Eden felt her stomach sink.

"I'm a little nervous about how I'll fit into your world." Jamie stood and began to pace nervously. "I have to admit that when I've been in Al's home, that way of living is a little intimidating. What will your friends think of me?"

"Jamie, I don't have many friends, and frankly, I couldn't care less what they think. I think I know better than most that all the trappings of wealth mean little when you're alone." Eden stood and pulled Jamie close to her. "Just give me a chance, and I promise you'll see that I'm not the rich brat you think I am."

Jamie stroked Eden's face and smiled. "I never truly thought of you as a rich brat...just a brat."

"How do you know that Miss Spencer didn't make the call to Laura McManus?" Detective Marchand asked between bites of his steak.

Detective Salamoni rubbed her glass against her temple, feeling her headache intensify. "Because she's the one who brought it to my attention, and frankly, I don't think she's lying."

"I don't think she's lying either, but we have both her and Patton's prints on the phone. Holly Patton is missing and presumed dead, so unless McManus spills the beans, we can't rule out Spencer."

"I'm still sticking with my theory that Holly Patton is alive and was working with McManus." Detective Salamoni polished off the remainder of her drink and motioned for another.

Detective Marchand wiped his mouth and leaned back in his seat, feeling full from his meal. His portly stomach still touched the table. "You heard what the DA said. McManus's attorneys will tear your theory apart. They're going to do their best to discredit Spencer. I'm not saying McManus will walk, but a jury may buy into the reluctant accomplice defense. And, Melanie, you're putting a lot of stock into what Jamie Spencer is telling you. Have you even considered that she may have been working with McManus and killed Holly Patton? She may be the bad guy."

"Eden Carlton said Spencer was with her the whole time. She couldn't have sneaked out, killed Holly Patton, and dumped her body in Florida."

"First, Carlton was admittedly out of her head for a while. Second, Spencer could've had an accomplice," Marchand argued.

"I hate it when you play devil's advocate, Dale," Detective Salamoni replied bitterly.

"I just want to make sure your head is in the right place. These aren't your typical Joe Schmoes; these people are wealthy and have some very high-profile attorneys, not to mention the media interest. I really think what the DA suggested earlier is a viable alternative."

"Drop it and let a murderer go free?" Detective Salamoni asked bitterly.

"If we don't push this phone call, we don't have to involve Spencer, which you don't want to do. McManus's attorneys aren't going to bring it up because that may link their client to an accomplice who could sway the whole case, so the best thing for all is to let this drop."

Detective Salamoni scrubbed her face in frustration. "I know, I know, play the game and everyone's happy."

Jamie lay on the sofa with her head in Eden's lap while Eden ran her fingers through her hair. "I think we've cleared the air on just about everything, don't you?" she asked, looking up into Eden's eyes.

Eden chuckled. "Just about? Is there more we need to discuss?"

THE TAKING OF EDEN

Jamie sat up and shifted so she was facing Eden. "Well, there's one more thing I need to know. Do we start dating or do we pick up where we left off?"

Eden cocked an eyebrow. "That depends on where you think we left off."

Jamie smiled seductively. "I think we left off when I fell asleep in your arms that night."

Eden grinned. "So this is where you get up and cook me breakfast and tell me how great I was?"

Jamie leaned up and kissed Eden, nibbling on her bottom lip before pulling away. "No, this is where you refresh my memory about how good you are."

"I'd carry you up to bed, but I don't think you want me trying to make it up that ladder," Eden said breathlessly.

Jamie nibbled at Eden's neck. "I've had this fantasy since we left this place about us, a blanket, and a moonlit night. I have a bottle of wine stashed in my car, and if you'll climb up to the loft and get a blanket, I'll make the climb worth your while," Jamie said with a seductive tone that sent Eden scrambling up the ladder.

Jamie strolled out to her SUV and retrieved the bottle of Cabernet, as Eden appeared behind her with blankets and a grin. "I hope you don't mind sharing. I threw my bag on top of the other glass and broke it," Jamie said as she took Eden by the hand and led her to the spot she had spent many nights dreaming about near the lake. The sun was just setting and the mood was perfect.

She watched as Eden spread one of the blankets out on the ground with shaking hands. She remembered how brazen Eden was the first time they slept together, and now the cocky brunette seemed nervous. A grin tugged at Jamie's lips as she watched Eden fumble nervously with her shoes as she took a spot in the little nest she'd made.

"Are you nervous about being caught out here in the open or is it me?" Jamie pressed the corkscrew into the top of the bottle.

Eden struggled to look casual as she tucked the other blanket behind her head and lay back. "This just feels like the first time, and I'm hoping I don't do anything to screw it up," Eden responded sheepishly.

Jamie took a sip from the glass before passing it to Eden, who emptied it and passed it back to her. "I feel a little better now," she said with a grin.

Jamie set the glass next to the bottle and curled up next to Eden, resting her head on her shoulder. "I feel like I'm dreaming all this again. Did you dream of me while we were apart?"

Eden sighed. "I tried my best not to think of you, it was just too painful. But every night when I slept, you filled my dreams. And when I awoke in the morning, I swear I could smell you." Eden ran her fingers through Jamie's blonde tresses.

"Everyone has a scent that is so uniquely them. It doesn't have anything to do with your perfume or shampoo; it's just your smell. I remember being so sick, and even though I was too weak to open my eyes, I could smell you, and it comforted me because I knew you were close by."

Touched by Eden's words, Jamie leaned up and kissed her tenderly, savoring the soft feel of the lips she had missed so desperately. Eden wove her fingers deeper into Jamie's hair and pulled her close, moaning as Jamie's tongue slipped over her bottom lip.

When they broke the kiss, Eden gently pushed Jamie away. "I want to watch you undress."

Jamie chuckled. "You've seen me undress. I remember the way you stared at me that morning I helped you shower."

Eden sat up and tugged at the bottom of Jamie's sweater. "Yes, but that was different. I want to feel free to look at you."

Jamie stood and pulled her sweater over her head, as Eden lay back on the blanket watching. So much was reflected in her eyes—love, adoration, and desire—that Jamie shivered at the intensity. She shrugged out of the T-shirt, silently cursing the layers that prolonged the process. Eden's eyes widened as she unclasped her bra and let it fall to the ground.

Eden clutched unconsciously at the blanket beneath her as each layer of clothing was discarded until Jamie stood before her completely naked. "Come here," Eden softly ordered as

Jamie slowly dropped to her knees and straddled her body, holding her gaze the entire time.

Gray-blue eyes closed as fingertips grazed over smooth skin. Memories of the first time she touched the soft body flooded Eden's thoughts, filling her with a desire she fought to keep at bay. She wanted to savor each second and touch of the gift that had been offered to her. Her hands trembled as she ran her fingertips over the velvet skin of Jamie's stomach, feeling the muscles beneath the skin twitch under her touch. Eden exhaled the breath she had been intentionally holding, wanting nothing to impede what she was feeling.

Jamie watched Eden's brow furrow with concentration as she explored her skin. Jamie unbuttoned Eden's shirt and traced her fingers over her skin, slowly stoking the fire within her. When her hands made their way to exposed skin, Eden suddenly grabbed her hands. "Please don't touch me; I don't want to lose my concentration," Eden pleaded as she sat up and pulled Jamie closer to her.

Jamie wrapped her legs around Eden's waist and buried her face into soft brown hair. "I won't, but please don't deny me that pleasure when you're done," Jamie whispered breathlessly as Eden's tongue traced her collarbone.

"You can do anything you want to me, but for now just let me enjoy you," Eden said as she dipped her head and slowly circled Jamie's nipple with her tongue. Jamie leaned her head back, lost in the sensation, gritting her teeth and moaning into the dusky sky. The fall air nipped at her skin as the warmth of Eden's mouth encircled her nipple, making her tremble.

Eden nibbled and sucked at the tender flesh as Jamie's moans and whimpers fanned the flames of her desire higher and higher. Needing more, she gently forced Jamie onto her back, giving her more access to the body she had craved for so long.

Jamie wove her fingers into Eden's hair as she kissed her way down a trembling stomach. Her murmurs of pleasure teased Jamie's ears as her tongue and mouth teased her skin. Jamie's breath left her as she felt Eden's mouth graze her inner thigh. And when she felt Eden's tongue press into her, her eyes opened wide, barely taking notice of the starry sky above her.

Eden's bare toes flexed in the grass as she pushed her upper body harder against Jamie. She wrapped her arms around flexing thighs as she used her tongue and mouth to make Jamie squirm beneath her. Her lover's pleas washed over her in waves and settled in the pit of her stomach as her own excitement built and threatened to take over. Jamie's body arched off the blanket, and every muscle in her body went rigid. The shuddering cry came all too soon for Eden, who was enraptured with the task at hand.

Jamie bit at her lip as Eden refused to be pushed away. Avoiding the tender spot, she kissed and nibbled until Jamie began to feel another orgasm build.

Eden lightly ran her tongue over the swollen pebble of flesh and groaned with satisfaction as Jamie's body arched again off the ground for the second time. Only when she felt Jamie's body go limp with exhaustion did she stop, still longing to take her to the same heights.

"Come here," Jamie rasped hoarsely as she pulled Eden's body against her. "I want these off," she whispered as she tugged at Eden's clothing. Eden shrugged out of her sweater and jeans and groaned with delight as she snuggled against Jamie's hot skin.

"Okay, I'm ready to admit how wonderful you are, but I'm not cooking breakfast," Jamie grinned. "I'm too relaxed and I have other things on my mind." She rose up on one elbow and looked down at Eden, who lay grinning next to her.

"I'm pretty content right now," Eden purred as she ran her fingertips down Jamie's stomach before being stopped.

"Are you trying to distract me?" Jamie teased as she pushed Eden's hand away.

"Is that a bad thing?" Eden asked as Jamie ran her fingers over her stomach, making her pant.

Jamie smiled and pushed Eden's hands down on the blanket. "Remember your promise, I get to do anything I want right now."

Eden clutched handfuls of blanket as Jamie ran her fingertips lightly up and down her body.

Jamie leaned down and whispered in Eden's ear as she hooked one of her legs around Eden's, holding it firmly, and dipped her hand between Eden's legs. "Keep your eyes on me."

Eden hissed between clenched teeth when she felt Jamie's fingers dip inside of her.

Jamie watched Eden's face bathed in moonlight as she slowly stroked her. "Look at me, Eden," she reminded softly when her lover's eyes drifted shut.

Eden's eyes opened slowly as Jamie's fingers circled her clit. This level of intimacy was not something Eden was accustomed to. Even when she was with Jamie the last time, it had been about sex. This time, she was making love, and the intensity of it was unnerving.

"Relax and give in to me," Jamie whispered, looking into her eyes.

Eden stared back, her breathing coming in pants and gasps as Jamie's hand stroked her.

"What did you enjoy the most while you were making love to me?" Jamie asked softly.

"The sounds you made and the way you felt...against my mouth."

Jamie watched as Eden's eyes closed and her lip trembled as she inhaled and held her breath. The look on her face was a mix of ecstasy and pain as the orgasm overtook her until she finally went limp in Jamie's arms.

When Eden's breathing began to calm, Jamie pulled the blanket over them and pulled Eden close. "I love you," she whispered against Eden's head as she drifted off to sleep.

Chapter Sixteen

"Jamie, you need to go get Eden from the garage," Ann huffed as she set the empty snack tray on the kitchen counter.

"Why?" Jamie and her mother asked in unison.

"Dad has her out there with his poker buddies, and she's already been corrupted."

"Are they playing with real money again?" Barbara Spencer asked as she peeked in the oven to admire her turkey.

"Yes, and Eden's losing her shirt. She already has her watch on the table," Ann said with a chuckle.

"Mom, I'm going to need your help with this." Jamie grabbed her mother by the elbow and led her to the garage.

Eden and Al sat side by side, both with a cigar in their mouths when Jamie and her mother entered the room. "Tommy Spencer!" Barbara barked. "There will be no gambling in my house on Christmas Eve!"

"Six sets of guilty eyes looked back at her. "Tommy and Eden, you get in this house. Al, you too," Barbara commanded as people began to scramble. "The rest of you need to be home with your families, not hiding in here and losing your money."

The room was cleared in a matter of minutes. Jamie and Barbara could hear Al, Eden, and Tommy laughing as they escaped into the house. Jamie plucked Eden's watch from the table. "What are you going to do with the money?" Jamie asked as she scooped up the bills.

"What I always do," Barbara replied with a smile. "I go shopping, and your father has to settle up with his buddies."

Jamie chuckled. "I don't think you have your bluff in on Eden and Al like you do Dad."

"The key is that he has to live with me. Work on your bluffing skills, darling, they'll come in handy with Eden," Barbara said with a smirk.

"You like her, Mom?" Jamie asked seriously.

"We've only known her for two days and we adore her. Your dad and I were talking about her this morning. She's a genuine person, and it's obvious that she loves you dearly."

Jamie pulled her mom in for a hug. "Thanks, Mom, she's very important to me."

"I know, sweetie, and I wish the best for you both."

"Mom…" Ann poked her head in the door. "Better get in here quick, Dad's looking for the blender. He's ready to make margaritas."

Barbara grimaced as she looked down at her watch. "It's only eleven in the morning. I'm going to choke that man!"

Ann looked at Jamie with an evil grin. "Now that I have them all riled up, I'm getting the hell out of here. I was supposed to be at Tim's parents' an hour ago."

"Give Kaitlyn a kiss for me and be back here on time this evening," Jamie said as she shoved her sister out the door.

By late afternoon, Ann returned with her husband, Tim, and their daughter, Kaitlyn, after spending some time with Tim's parents. Kaitlyn charged into the den and was lavished with kisses and hugs from her grandparents. Spying her favorite aunt Jamie, she launched herself into her lap, then studied Eden curiously.

"Who?" she asked as she pointed her tiny finger in Eden's direction.

"That's Eden, say hi," Jamie said as she smiled at them both.

"Hi," Kaitlyn said as she crawled into Eden's lap and played with her hair. "You hair fritty," Kaitlyn said as she tugged on the dark strands.

"Translated, that means she thinks your hair is pretty," Jamie said with a giggle, as Eden looked at her curiously. "Everyone around here is blonde, so you're very unique."

"Oh, well, your hair is pretty, too," Eden said as she ran her fingers through the tight blonde curls.

"Kaitlyn, it's time to pass out the gifts," Ann called, causing the tiny tot to jump up and run to the tree.

"This one is for Eden," Tommy whispered to his granddaughter, who took it and returned to Eden. "This for you," she said happily as she took her place back in Eden's lap.

Jamie gave her a nudge. "You have more gifts to pass out."

"Don't want to," Kaitlyn said as she returned to Eden's hair.

"Since the spider monkey is busy grooming Eden, I'll have to take up her slack," Ann said as she grabbed a few gifts from under the tree.

"Are you okay?" Jamie asked as Kaitlyn filled her hands full of Eden's hair.

"As long as she doesn't decide to pull my hair out," Eden replied with a grin.

As per custom, the Spencer children always gave their parents gag gifts before the real ones. Barbara and Tommy Spencer sat side by side as Barbara peeled away the wrapping from the first gift given by Ann and Jamie.

Al tucked himself away in a comfortable chair watching the proceedings. He marveled at how much the two sisters looked like their mother. Barbara Spencer was a few pounds heavier but could have easily passed for an older sister with her young looks.

Ann obviously had gotten her reddish-blonde hair from her father, but neither of the girls had been blessed with his height.

He glanced over at Eden, who sat at Jamie's side with Kaitlyn still perched in her lap. There was a happiness on her face that he had never seen before. That in itself was the best Christmas gift he could have ever gotten. He sank back into the warmth of the chair hoping that when it was his time to leave this life, Eden would always be surrounded by the love of the woman sitting next to her.

Laughter broke out as Barbara pulled a feather boa and a risqué negligee out of the box. "Oh, it's a very merry Christmas indeed," Tommy teased at her side. His box contained skimpy underwear with an elephant's face on the front with a suspicious trunk. He quickly tucked it behind his back before Kaitlyn caught sight of it.

"We don't want to hear about the fun you both have with those," Jamie said, causing her mother's blush to deepen.

"All right, you've had your fun at our expense, now, everyone else, open your gifts," Barbara told the group.

Al groaned with delight when he opened one of his gifts and found a nice bottle of brandy and expensive cigars from the Spencers. Eden topped it off with a new smoking jacket since Al always felt it necessary to be formal in his own home.

Eden broke into a fit of laughter when she opened her gift from the Spencers. Jamie looked at her bewildered; she knew her parents had given Eden a robe for Christmas, but she was a little concerned that Eden found it so funny. Barbara and Tommy were laughing right along with Eden, and when Jamie looked at Ann, she was laughing, too.

Jamie narrowed her eyes at Eden. "What's in that box?"

Eden held up two pictures of Jamie. One was taken when she was an infant, lying bare-bottomed on a blanket. The second was taken when she was in the second grade and her two front teeth were missing. To make matters worse, she had gum stuck in her hair.

"Your dad and I figured we should be able to give a few gag gifts ourselves," Barbara laughed unrepentantly.

Ann's husband had already opened his gift and was holding a cassette tape with a curious expression on his face.

"And, Tim, on that cassette, you'll hear Ann performing a song she wrote when she was six. I think it's called 'Fireball,'" Barbara said, trying to catch her breath between fits of laughter.

Ann looked horrified. "Oh, my God, Tim! You give me that!" Tim leaped from the chair and ran toward the stereo with Ann hot on his heels.

"You were really cute as a child," Eden said with a laugh, as she nudged Jamie in the ribs.

"I went to sleep with gum in my mouth the night before school pictures, and I guess the result was obvious."

Eden tucked the pictures into her shirt pocket. "I'm going to frame these," she said with a wicked grin.

"My family is a little nutty, I hope you're not getting the wrong impression of us."

"I think they're wonderful," Eden said as the first few bars of Ann's infamous song blared through the den.

Ann and Tim were in a wrestling match over the stereo and Kaitlyn joined in, fighting on both sides of the good-humored battle.

"My gift for you is kind of personal, do you mind if I give it to you a little later?"

"Mine is too," Jamie said with a wink. "We'll celebrate our way tonight when we're alone."

Dinner was a much louder affair than Eden was accustomed to with everyone talking over one another, but she enjoyed it nonetheless. Ann leaned over and whispered in her ear. "I told you that you'd be here for the holidays, didn't I?"

Eden clanked her glass with Ann's. "Here's to your faith," she toasted with a smile.

"I'm glad you stuck with my sister in her mule stage. She's wrapped around your little finger, and from the looks of it, you're wrapped just as tight," Ann said with a grin. "You're good for each other."

"She's the best thing that has ever happened to me, aside from Al," Eden said, looking up at Al, who sat across the table with Kaitlyn in his lap. "I don't know what I would've done without them."

"Jamie's lucky to have you," Ann said as she pulled Eden in for a hug. Jamie watched the exchange with a cheerful heart.

After everyone settled in for the night, Jamie and Eden celebrated being alone for the first time that day with a bottle of champagne in front of the fireplace in the den.

"Your family really went out of their way to make me feel welcome," Eden said after taking a sip from her glass. "And Al too."

Jamie pecked Eden on the lips and snuggled closer to her. "They really like you and Al, and I'm especially fond of you. That's why I got you this," Jamie said as she tugged the last present from under the tree.

Eden grinned as she unwrapped the box and pulled open the lid. Inside was a brown leather jacket and sitting on top was a miniature gold skeleton key attached to a matching chain.

"The jacket is to replace the one I ruined when I caused you to fall into the lake at the cabin. The key is just a symbol that means you hold the key to my heart," Jamie said with a smile.

"I love it, thank you," she said as she kissed Jamie lightly on the lips. Eden slipped her hand into the pocket of her robe and pulled out a small rectangular box. "My gift has a similar meaning."

Jamie took the box from Eden's hand and unwrapped it, revealing a velvet case. "I have a feeling that I don't deserve whatever is inside," she said nervously.

Eden chuckled. "Well, honey, you're stuck with it for life."

Jamie opened the lid and found two simple gold bands.

"These are symbols, too. If you choose to put your ring on, it means you're willing to be stuck with me for life," Eden explained nervously with a grin.

Jamie looked up at Eden with a smile. "And if you put the other ring on your finger, then you're stuck with me, just like that?"

"Unless you'd like to wait and have some sort of ceremony, but I remembered you saying one time that that wasn't your cup of tea," Eden replied, unsure if she had gone about it the wrong way.

Jamie plucked the larger of the two bands from the box. "I'd like to put yours on," she said with a tear in her eye.

Eden held up her left hand and Jamie slipped the ring onto her finger. Without a word, Eden took the other band out of the box and held it up for Jamie to see. "It's inscribed."

Jamie looked at the inscription as Eden held it. *My savior, my love* was carved into the band. "You saved me in more ways than one, Jamie. You saved my life, and you became my life," Eden said softly as she slid the ring onto Jamie's finger.

Jamie sniffed back a sob as she looked down at their joined hands. "I'm so glad you did this, this way. It's just for us, no one else. And I'm so glad you thought I deserved to be stuck with you for life," she said with a laugh.

"I warned you that you would be stuck with it before you opened the box," Eden said with a chuckle, then her expression turned serious. "I meant it when I said it's for life, there's no other who has made me feel the way you do. I want you to be my partner in all things."

Jamie lifted Eden's left hand to her lips and kissed the ring finger. "Till death do us part."

Eden stood and tugged Jamie to her feet. "We have a honeymoon to celebrate," she said with a grin as she led Jamie to their bedroom.

Jamie chewed her lip, trying her best to be quiet as Eden kissed her way down her stomach. "I'm looking forward to not having to be quiet," she whispered.

Eden rubbed her face across the softness of Jamie's skin. "I think we should enjoy not having to be quiet in your new house."

Jamie ran her fingers through the dark waves of hair that spread across her stomach. "Are you saying you want us to live in my house and not yours?"

Eden looked up with a smile. "I love it there, but if you want, we can find somewhere new."

"I love my place and I'm more than thrilled to know you like it, too," Jamie said with a sigh as Eden began kissing trails down her skin again.

Eden paused and looked up. "We could build a deck on the back by the glass doors, and I'd like to remodel the garage out back and make it into a game room."

Jamie pressed her finger to Eden's lips. "Can we discuss this another time? My brain is elsewhere at the moment."

Eden chuckled and began tracing patterns on Jamie's skin with her fingertip. "If this were the front of the house," she whispered as she ran her finger in a straight line across Jamie's stomach, "we could build flower beds that come all the way out to here." She grinned as she dipped her fingers between Jamie's legs and stroked lightly over the moist skin.

"Okay, sure, flower beds," Jamie purred.

Eden sat up and urged Jamie onto her stomach. She ran her fingers lightly down the skin of her back. "Imagine this as the backyard."

Jamie groaned. "I'm having a hard time with that mental image at the moment."

Eden traced a square across Jamie's back. "Now this is the deck." She ran her nails lightly across Jamie's backside. "Here and here will be the other flower beds."

Jamie groaned again. "Eden, I don't give a damn about the gardening, get inside the house already."

Eden laughed out loud before she caught herself. "Patience, I'm not nearly finished with the prep work."

The next morning, Kaitlyn charged down the hall screaming at the top of her lungs just before the sun rose. Santa had been there, and a new tricycle sat in front of the tree. Everyone in the house groaned as the toddler commanded everyone to come see her toys.

Jamie and Eden were the last to leave their room since they had only gotten two hours sleep. Jamie glanced into her parents' room to see if they had already risen. She stopped suddenly and tugged hard on Eden's hand, causing Eden to stop and look at her. "Oh, my God, Eden," Jamie said as a grin split her face. She pulled Eden into the bedroom where feathers littered the floor.

"Mom wore the boa last night," Jamie said with a squeal. "I can't wait to tell Ann!"

Eden chuckled and picked up a handful of feathers. "Eww, Jamie, your dad plucked your mom last night."

Chapter Seventeen

"Eden, do you know where I put my keys?" Jamie asked as she frantically dug through her purse.

"How would I know where your keys are when you're the last person who had them?" Eden replied testily as she pulled her coat from the closet.

"I was hoping you noticed where I put them," Jamie said as she marched off into the kitchen.

Eden huffed and dropped her coat in the middle of the floor and made her way to the bedroom. Digging into the hamper, she found the jeans that Jamie wore the day before. She reached into the front pocket and grinned. "I found them," she called out.

Jamie raced into their bedroom, pulling off her shoes and tossing them into the closet. "I can't wear these," she said as she rummaged through her shoeboxes.

Eden looked at her watch and put her hand on her hip. "Why not?"

Jamie looked at her like she was crazy. "You don't wear open-toed shoes before Easter."

Eden rolled her eyes. "That's the dumbest thing I've ever heard." She looked at her watch again impatiently. "We're going to be late for the trial, and since I've been subpoenaed, I would like to at least get there on time."

Jamie looked at her outfit in the mirror and grimaced. "This outfit makes me look fat!"

"You're not fat and you look fine. Can we please go now?"

Jamie pushed Eden through the doorway. "I'm right behind you. Did you remember to turn the coffeepot off?"

Eden spun on one heel and looked at Jamie.

"Don't roll your eyes at me, you left it on yesterday and nearly burned our house down."

Eden tugged Jamie down the hall and through the front door. "That's why tomorrow we're going to buy one with an automatic shutoff."

"You drive," Jamie said as she tossed her keys to Eden, who opened Jamie's door for her, then walked around the SUV and climbed into the driver's seat.

"When we get home this afternoon, I'm going to finish the flower beds," Eden said as she backed out of the driveway.

Jamie never heard a word she said, she was too busy fussing with her makeup and hair.

Eden stopped the vehicle in the middle of the road. "What is going on with you today? Is this PMS? We can't PMS at the same time, someone will die."

"It's not that, I just feel like a slob today."

"You look amazing, but I've never seen you act like this. What's going on with you?" Eden asked as she stepped on the gas.

Jamie looked out the window for a moment, then looked back at Eden. "I don't want to look like a loser in front of Laura."

Eden chuckled and took Jamie's hand. "You don't think she's competition, do you?"

"You said you thought she was very attractive, and you did have a relationship with her." Jamie winced at her tone; she sounded like a petulant child even to her own ears.

"She's not the woman who holds my heart, though. That's reserved only for you." Eden squeezed Jamie's hand tightly. "The only face I care about seeing in that courtroom is yours."

The statuesque blonde was led into the courtroom and seated next to her attorneys, one of whom poured her a glass of water and whispered in her ear. Jamie stiffened, feeling jealousy and anger surge through her, seeing in person for the first time the woman responsible for her life being turned upside down. Eden felt the tension coming off her partner in waves and discreetly took her hand as they waited for the hearing to begin.

Laura McManus looked over her shoulder and searched the crowd until her eyes landed on Eden. Jamie gripped her hand so tightly that Eden's fingertips blanched. Eden glared back at Laura, contempt displayed on her face.

Laura's eyes slowly moved and settled on Jamie. Both blondes locked eyes and a sneer tugged at the corner of Laura's lips. Al, who sat on the other side of Jamie, watched the exchange and chuckled softly when Jamie mouthed, "mine," causing Laura to look away in disgust.

On the second day of the trial, Eden was called to the stand, and Jamie watched with pride as Eden fingered the gold band on her left hand each time she was asked a question, knowingly drawing Laura's attention to it.

Jamie glanced down at her left hand and looked at the matching band that encircled her finger, then back up at her partner. She had always thought that Eden was beautiful, but today she was stunning in her black business suit, which brought out the blue in her eyes. Her soft alto voice filled the courtroom as she confidently answered each question posed to her.

Jamie smiled as she remembered looking at Eden the day before when it had been her turn on the stand. Eden's eyes reflected the love she felt in her heart, and it calmed her as she was grilled by Laura's attorneys.

Laura played the part of the unwilling accomplice like a veteran actress. Tears flowed from her eyes as she looked at Eden and begged her for forgiveness. It was Eden's turn to hold tight to Jamie's hand, keeping her from disrupting the proceedings. Jamie hissed under her breath the entire time Laura spoke.

When the jury filed into the courtroom with the verdict, tension was running high and bounced off the walls like static electricity. The guilty verdict brought on shouts of joy, as the judge commanded control over the courtroom. The three-year sentence brought the same response, but instead of joy, it was gasps of disbelief.

Jamie held Eden's hand tightly after they went through security. Eden set her purse on a dingy table and took both of Jamie's hands. "I've got to do this."

"I know, and I'll be right here if you need me," Jamie said as she felt Eden's hands fall away from hers. She watched her partner walk across the room and take a seat in the booth. She was close enough to see Eden but too far away to hear what was being said. Jamie pulled out a chair and sat down.

Laura McManus sat on the other side of the glassed-in booth. She ran her fingers through her blonde hair, feeling ill at ease since her true hair color was beginning to show. She pulled some of the strands close to her face in a meager attempt to cover the dark patch around her eye. "You'll have to excuse my appearance; we don't have a decent salon in here," she joked as Eden stared at her through the glass.

"I really don't care about what you look like, Laura," Eden said coolly into the handset.

"Honey, I know what you must think of me, but I never meant it to go as far as it did," Laura pleaded.

"Cut the shit, you're not on the stand anymore, there's no jury here to play to. Just tell me what I did to deserve what you did to me," Eden snarled.

Laura's face turned cold. "Don't sit there and act like you didn't have a hand in this. If you wouldn't have been such a bitch and treated me like shit, this would've never happened. Because of you, I was easy prey for that con artist."

"Well, she's dead, and the jury never got to hear her side of the story. I'm sure your sentence would've been significantly longer if she hadn't killed herself," Eden said.

Laura threw back her head and laughed. "Susan was an idiot but wasn't nearly as dumb as you are." Laura's face turned cold again. "The real brain is somewhere living it up on your money right now as we speak."

Eden stared back at Laura as she tried to process what she was hearing.

"Dad used to love to rub my nose in his success," Laura continued. "One day while he was showing off one of his new clinics, I met her. She treated me like a lady, so unlike you, and I fell for it hook, line, and sinker." Laura paused and scrubbed at her face in frustration. "I didn't even realize it was her who took you from the clinic until a few days later."

"What the hell are you talking about?" Eden asked, refusing to believe what she was hearing.

"She held all the cards and left me and Susan to fend for ourselves. Right up to the last minute, I thought for sure she would come through for me, but that day in the airport when my nose was shoved into the wall and they read me my rights, I knew I had been screwed."

Eden slammed her hand down onto the counter, causing the guard to raise a brow. "This is just more of your bullshit!"

Laura grinned at Eden through the glass. "Tell me...is your little nurse as good to you as I was? She doesn't look very adventurous; does she bore you in the bedroom?"

"How did you get that black eye? Are your cellmates a little too adventurous in the showers?" Eden shot back.

Laura leaned back in her seat and smiled. "I get it better in here than I ever did with you, you're a lousy lay."

"Then you must enjoy having a broomstick rammed up your ass," Eden said with a grin.

"Two more minutes, McManus," the guard called out.

Laura leaned forward and placed both elbows on the counter. "Did you sleep with Holly, too? Tell me what she was like, I never had the pleasure. She just screwed me over."

"Holly is dead, so that just leaves you to rot in here alone," Eden sneered.

Laura smiled again and Eden realized at that moment that the woman whom she once thought was attractive was truly vile inside and out.

"They never found her body, and I'm certain they aren't even looking for her now. Just know that justice has not been served. She screwed you, just like she did me, and she's the one enjoying your money." Laura stood and prepared to be led back to her cell. "It was good to see you," she quipped snidely.

"Enjoy your rides on the broomstick," Eden said before hanging up her handset.

"Are you okay?" Jamie asked as Eden walked up and took her purse.

"I'm fine, but let's wait to get outside before we discuss anything further."

Eden took Jamie by the hand, and they went back through the same security checkpoints they had before. Eden filled her lungs with fresh air when they walked outside, relieved to be out of the oppressive atmosphere and the dirty feeling of being in such a place.

Detective Salamoni was poised in front of her car with her arms folded over her chest. "Well?" she asked with a knowing smirk.

"It went as easy as you said it would. She told me about Holly without me having to ask." Eden wrapped her arm over Jamie's shoulders as they slumped down.

"I just can't believe she did this, but in hindsight, it makes so much sense now—why she was so adamant about not going to the police when we took Eden that morning. I was too shaken to think rationally," Jamie said as she rubbed her temples.

"Don't knock yourself, Jamie. She really screwed with Susan and Laura's heads, too. She let them do all the dirty work and knocked them both off kilter when she took Eden and put the ball in her court. Laura had already secured the passports and the money, and Holly left the country without her. That's gotta rub Laura the wrong way, and she has three years with nothing but time to think about it."

Jamie smiled at Eden. "I'm not happy that it happened, but I'm thankful for what I took away from it all."

Detective Salamoni shook both their hands and thanked them for helping to get the confirmation she needed. "I have a lot of work ahead of me now, and I'll keep you both abreast of what I find on Holly."

"Well, what will we do with ourselves now that we've finished all the work on the yard and the house?" Eden said as they strolled lazily to their car.

Jamie grinned and took Eden by the hand. "I think we need a relaxing weekend, and I know of a little love nest in the woods that would be perfect for just that."

Epilogue

A gentle breeze blew in off the water, cooling overheated skin as she lay looking at the ugly scar on her arm. She had drawn the knife deeper than she intended, but she accomplished the desired effect when she left behind huge traces of her blood in the van.

Kelly Edgemont nearly bled to death as she waited to board the plane. Her wound was concealed under the sleeve of a heavy coat that was beginning to soak through with her blood. She handed her fake passport with shaking hands to the officials when she landed on the tropical island; true freedom was simply a checkpoint away.

Six months had passed since that horrible trip, and the scar was just beginning to really heal. She never liked the name Kelly, but then again, Laura wasn't very creative. The foolish blonde secured the fake passport and now Holly would have to learn to live with the name.

She smiled and waved at the well-built man five years her junior as he trimmed the sails of the boat that sliced through the blue water. His seduction was as easy as Laura's had been. Simply pretend to be in awe of their physical beauty and they were wrapped around her finger, sometimes so tightly it hurt. Laura was easier than any man Holly had ever met. She had never so much as kissed the woman, and with a few well-placed words and empty promises, she had the spoiled tramp eating out of her hand.

Occasionally, there were moments when she felt guilt for Jamie. She had been so trusting and willing to help someone in need that she fell into the plan without a hitch. The papers spoke of her heroism, so maybe she faired well after all, Holly thought to herself.

"Here's to you, Jamie," Holly said in toast as she raised her glass to the sea ahead. "I hope you and the rich bitch live happily ever after because this rich dead woman certainly is."

About the author

Born in 1965, Robin Alexander grew up in Baton Rouge, Louisiana, where she still resides. An avid reader of lesbian fiction, Robin decided to take the leap and try her hand at writing, which is now more than her favorite hobby. Other favorites are camping, snorkeling, and anything to do with the outdoors or the water. Robin approaches everything with a sense of humor, which is evident in her style of writing. To learn more about Robin and read some of her short stories, visit www.robinfic.com.

Other Intaglio Publications Titles

Accidental Love, by B. L. Miller, ISBN: 1-933113-11-1, Price: 18.15
What happens when love is based on deception? Can it survive discovering the truth?

Code Blue, by KatLyn, ISBN: 1-933113-09-X, Price: $16.95 - Thrown headlong into one of the most puzzling murder investigations in the Burgh's history, Logan McGregor finds that politics, corruption, money and greed aren't the only barriers she must break through in order to find the truth.

Counterfeit World, by Judith K. Parker, ISBN: 1-933113-32-4, Price: $15.25
The U.S. government has been privatized, religion has only recently been decriminalized, the World Government keeps the peace on Earth—when it chooses—and multi-world corporations vie for control of planets, moons, asteroids, and orbits for their space stations.

Crystal's Heart, by B. L. Miller & Verda Foster, ISBN: 1-933113-24-3, Price: $18.50 - Two women who have absolutely nothing in common, and yet when they become improbable housemates, are amazed to find they can actually live with each other. And not only live...

Gloria's Inn, by Robin Alexander, ISBN: 1-933113-01-4, Price: $14.95 - Hayden Tate suddenly found herself in a world unlike any other, when she inherited half of an inn nestled away on Cat Island in the Bahamas.

Graceful Waters, by B. L. Miller & Verda Foster, ISBN: 1-933113-08-1, Price: $17.25 - Joanna Carey, senior instructor at Sapling Hill wasn't looking for anything more than completing one more year at the facility and getting that much closer to her private dream, a small cabin on a quiet lake. She was tough, smart and she had a plan for her life.

Halls Of Temptation, by Katie P. Moore, ISBN: 978-1-933113-42-5, Price: $15.50 – A heartfelt romance that traces the lives of two young women from their teenage years into adulthood, through the struggles of maturity, conflict and love.

I Already Know The Silence Of The Storms, by N. M. Hill, ISBN: 1-933113-07-3, Price: $15.25 - I Already Know the Silence of the Storms is a map of a questor's journey as she traverses the tempestuous landscapes of heart, mind, body, and soul. Tossed onto paths of origins and destinations unbeknownst to her, she is enjoined by the ancients to cross chartless regions beset with want and need and desire to find the truth within.

Incommunicado, by N. M. Hill & J. P. Mercer, ISBN: 1-933113-10-3, Price: $15.25 - Incommunicado is a world of lies, deceit, and death along the U.S/Mexico border. Set within the panoramic beauty of the unforgiving Sonoran Desert, it is the story of two strong, independent women: Cara Vittore Cipriano, a lawyer who was born to rule the prestigious Cipriano Vineyards; and Jaquelyn "Jake" Biscayne, an FBI forensic pathologist who has made her work her life.

Infinite Pleasures, Stacia Seaman & Nann Dunne (Eds.), ISBN: 1-933113-00-6, Price: $18.99 - Hot, edgy, beyond-the-envelope erotica from over thirty of the best lesbian authors writing today. This no-holds barred, tell it like you wish it could be collection is guaranteed to rocket your senses into overload and ratchet your body up to high-burn.

Josie & Rebecca: The Western Chronicles, by Vada Foster & BL Miller, ISBN: 1-933113-38-3, Price: $18.99 - At the center of this story are two women; one a deadly gunslinger bitter from the injustices of her past, the other a gentle dreamer trying to escape the horrors of the present. Their destinies come together one fateful afternoon when the feared outlaw makes the choice to rescue a young woman in trouble. For her part, Josie Hunter considers the brief encounter at an end once the girl is safe, but Rebecca Cameron has other ideas....

Misplaced People, by C. G. Devize, ISBN: 1-933113-30-8, Price: $17.99 - On duty at a London hospital, American loner Striker West is drawn to an unknown woman, who, after being savagely attacked, is on the verge of death. Moved by a compassion she cannot explain, Striker spends her off time at the bedside of the comatose patient, reading and willing her to recover. Still trying to conquer her own demons which have taken her so far from home, Striker is drawn deeper into the web of intrigue that surrounds this woman.

Murky Waters, by Robin Alexander, ISBN: 1-933113-33-2, Price: $15.25 - Claire Murray thought she was leaving her problems behind when she accepted a new position within Suarez Travel and relocated to Baton Rouge. Her excitement quickly diminishes when her mysterious stalker makes it known that there is no place Claire can hide. She is instantly attracted to the enigmatic Tristan Delacroix, who becomes more of a mystery to her every time they meet. Claire is thrust into a world of fear, confusion, and passion that will ultimately shake the foundations of all she once believed.

Picking Up The Pace, by Kimberly LaFontaine, ISBN: 1-933113-41-3, Price: 15.50 - Who would have thought a 25-year-old budding journalist could stumble across a story worth dying for in quiet Fort Worth, Texas? Angie Mitchell certainly doesn't and neither do her bosses. While following an investigative lead for the Tribune, she heads into the seediest part of the city to discover why homeless people are showing up dead with no suspects for the police to chase.

Southern Hearts, by Katie P Moore, ISBN: 1-933113-28-6, Price: $16.95 - For the first time since her father's passing three years prior, Kari Bossier returns to the south, to her family's stately home on the emerald banks of the bayou Teche, and to a mother she yearns to understand.

Storm Surge, by KatLyn, ISBN: 1-933113-06-5, Price: $16.95 - FBI Special Agent Alex Montgomery would have given her life in the line of duty, but she lost something far more precious when she became the target of ruthless drug traffickers. Recalled to Jacksonville to aid the local authorities in infiltrating the same deadly drug ring, she has a secret agenda--revenge. Despite her unexpected involvement with Conner Harris, a tough, streetwise detective who has dedicated her life to her job at the cost of her own personal happiness, Alex vows to let nothing--and no one--stand in the way of exacting vengeance on those who took from her everything that mattered.

These Dreams, by Verda Foster, ISBN: 1-933113-12-X, Price: $15.75 - Haunted from childhood by visions of a mysterious woman she calls, Blue Eyes, artist Samantha McBride is thrilled when a friend informs her that she's seen a woman who bears the beautiful face she has immortalized on canvas and dreamed about for so long. Thrilled by the possibility that Blue Eyes might be a flesh and blood person, Samantha sets out to find her, certain the woman must be her destiny.

The Chosen, by Verda H Foster, ISBN: 978-1-933113-25-8, Price: 15.25 - animals. That's the way it's always been. But the slaves are waiting for the coming of The Chosen One, the prophesied leader who will take them out of their bondage.

The Cost Of Commitment, by Lynn Ames, ISBN: 1-933113-02-2, Price: $16.95 Kate and Jay want nothing more than to focus on their love. But as Kate settles in to a new profession, she and Jay become caught up in the middle of a deadly scheme—pawns in a larger game in which the stakes are nothing less than control of the country.

The Last Train Home, by Blayne Cooper, ISBN: 1-933113-26-X, Price: $17.75 One cold winter's night in Manhattan's Lower East side, tragedy strikes the Chisholm family. Thrown together by fate and disaster, Virginia "Ginny" Chisholm meets Lindsay Killian, a street-smart drifter who spends her days picking pockets and riding the rails. Together, the young women embark on a desperate journey that spans from the slums of New York City to the Western Frontier, as Ginny tries to reunite her family, regardless of the cost.

The Price of Fame, by Lynn Ames, ISBN: 1-933113-04-9, Price: $16.75 - When local television news anchor Katherine Kyle is thrust into the national spotlight, it sets in motion a chain of events that will change her life forever. Jamison "Jay" Parker is an intensely career-driven Time magazine reporter; she has experienced love once, from afar, and given up on finding it again...That is, until circumstance and an assignment bring her into contact with her past.

The Gift, by Verda Foster, ISBN: 1-933113-03-0, Price: $15.35 - Detective Rachel Todd doesn't believe in Lindsay Ryan's visions of danger, even when the horrifying events Lindsay predicted come true. That mistake could cost more than one life before this rollercoaster ride is over. Verda Foster's The Gift is just that – a well-paced, passionate saga of suspense, romance, and the amazing bounty of family, friends, and second chances. From the first breathless page to the last, a winner.

The Value of Valor, by Lynn Ames, ISBN: 1-933113-04-9, Price: $16.75
Katherine Kyle is the press secretary to the president of the United States. Her lover, Jamison Parker, is a respected writer for Time magazine. Separated by unthinkable tragedy, the two must struggle to survive against impossible odds…

With Every Breath, by Alex Alexander, ISBN: 1-933113-39-1, Price: $15.25
Abigail Dunnigan wakes to a phone call telling her of the brutal murder of her former lover and dear friend. A return to her hometown for the funeral soon becomes a run for her life, not only from the murderer but also from the truth about her own well-concealed act of killing to survive during a war. As the story unfolds, Abby confesses her experiences in Desert Storm and becomes haunted with the past as the bizarre connection between then and now reveals itself. While the FBI works to protect her and apprehend the murderer, the murderer works to push Abby over the mental edge with their secret correspondence.

Intaglio Publication's Forthcoming Releases

Coming 2006

January
Illusionist, by Fran Heckrotte, ISBN: 1-933113-31-6
Journey's End, By LJ Maas, ISBN: 1-933113-45-6

February
Romance for LIFE, Lori L. Lake & Tara Young, Eds, ISBN: 1-933113-59-6,
Private Dancer, by T. J. Vertigo, ISBN: 1-933113-58-8
Define Destiny, by J. M. Dragon, ISBN: 1-933113-56-1
Journey's Of Discoveries, by Ellis Paris Ramsay, ISBN: 1-933113-43-X

March
Tumbleweed Fever, By LJ Maas, ISBN: 1-933113-51-0
Prairie Fire, By LJ Maas, ISBN: 1-933113-47-2
Compensation, by S. Anne Gardner, ISBN: 1-933113-57-X 2006
Assignment Sunrise, by I Christie, ISBN: 1-933113-40-5

April
She Waits, by M. K. Sweeney, ISBN: 1-933113-55-3
Meridio's Daughter, By LJ Maas, ISBN: 1-933113-48-0

June
Lilith, by Fran Heckrotte, ISBN: 1-933113-50-2
The Flipside of Desire, by Lynn Ames, ISBN: 1-933113-60-X
The Petal of the Rose, by LJ Maas, ISBN: 1-933113-49-9

November
Times Fell Hand, By LJ Maas, ISBN: 1-933113-52-9

Printed in the United States
66174LVS00003B/157-165

9 781933 113531